MCCULLOUGH'S JAMBOREE BOOK 4

KATHI S. BARTON

This is a work of fiction. Names, characters, places, and incidents are products of the author's imagination or are used fictitiously and are not to be construed as real. Any resemblance to actual events, locations, organizations, or persons, living or dead, is entirely coincidental.

World Castle Publishing, LLC
Pensacola, Florida
Copyright © Kathi S. Barton 2017
Paperback ISBN: 9781629898308
eBook ISBN: 9781629898315
First Edition World Castle Publishing, LLC, November 13, 2017
http://www.worldcastlepublishing.com

Cover: Karen Fuller
Editor: Maxine Bringenberg

Chapter 1

Larson looked at the headlines again. There was something so final about it that it hurt his heart to think that his friend was gone. Not just him, but his wife of twenty years as well.

Thomas and Donna Simmons had been found on an inflatable boat three days ago. Defensive injuries were all over their bodies, as well as several gunshot wounds that had more than likely had them suffering all the way to the end.

The newspaper hadn't given him as many details as Lauren had, but the paper had said that their deaths — murders — were being looked into. And where their boat had disappeared to. They had been shot in the head, both of them, and put on a dingy, he thought it was called.

"I'm sorry." He nodded at Lauren when she spoke. "I have some people looking into things since there are a lot of unexplained events. Also, and I don't know if you know him well, but their partner is saying some pretty damning things about you."

"Me? What does he think I did to them?" She said it was about money. "I was his investor and nothing more. I mean, we were friends too, but I never borrowed anything from his partner. The last time we spoke, he asked me to sell off some stock that he had and I did. It's all recorded too."

"Hang onto it...the recordings, I mean. The partner is saying that a week after Tom and his wife went away, you called him and told him that there was a deal just too good to pass up. He in turn told you that Tom was away and that he didn't make those sorts of decisions. But you insisted." Larson shook his head and told her that the partner had called him. "Well, like I said, hang onto those recordings. Also, you should think about closing up for a couple of days."

"Why?" She told him. "You think he's going to make trouble for me? That somehow, he can tell others that I'm a cheat and a liar? Why would he do that? I didn't do anything wrong."

"I know that, but you know how people can be. They're untrusting and will latch onto anything that they can to make someone else have less than them. It's the way the world works. As much as it sucks, you know as well as I that it does happen."

His phone rang then and he answered it, but almost as soon as the man on the other end, Harley Wells, said his name, he made sure that things were being recorded. And he put it on speaker phone so that Lauren could hear as well.

"Mr. Wells, I didn't expect to hear from you. Did you need some investing done?" Lauren slid a note to him about warning the other man he was being recorded. "You did listen to the options, didn't you? I mean, this is a very good place to have your money grow."

"Yes, I listened to all the options. Is this your way of asking me if I know that I'm being recorded? Besides, you can't use it, not now that I've put it out there that you're being sued by me. Anyway, I want you to know that I want that money back, and the shares put back where they were." He asked him how he thought he couldn't use the recordings. "Because I'll just say that I didn't call you. That you've doctored this whole thing, much like you did for my partner. He shouldn't have sold off that stock. I was hoping to use it."

All sorts of things jumped into Larson's mind, but looking at Lauren, he knew better than to say anything to Wells. Instead, he read the next note that she slid over to him. He didn't want to ask but she pointed to it again.

"Did you kill off Tom and his wife? For their shares?" Wells said that he had and that he'd do it again, but he'd be more careful this time. "Careful how? I'm assuming that you think you're the beneficiary to their estate."

"I will be." He laughed again. "Thomas do Jenny think October left me Vince." Larson asked him what he was doing when he started just saying words with no rhyme or reason to them. Lauren sliced her fingers over her throat and he hung up.

"I don't know what just happened here." She nodded, but he could see by the look on her face that she was worried. Or thinking. Either one of them, he wasn't too happy about. "Lauren, please tell me that you're going to figure this out."

"Oh I am. And you don't have to worry too much about him. I'd steer clear of him for sure, but I'd not be answering my phone for the next week or so." He asked her if that would make him sound guilty. "Perhaps, but in the end you'll be fine."

"And that garble of words, what was that?" She told him he was making words to sound as if he'd made a tape of their conversation. "Why would he need to do that? I mean, I'd not even have the first clue about that."

"But I would." He asked her what she meant, thinking that he knew what she was saying but wanting her to confirm it. "If I were in a position to use a recording of someone's voice to get them caught, then yes, I'd do it. And he would know that. It's no secret to anyone now as to what I'm capable of. Everyone thinks I work with the president. That I've gone out of my way to make sure that he's safe. Then there is the added fact that I made sure that our former president went to jail for a very long time."

"Why me? Why is he coming after me? I didn't do anything that wasn't asked of me. I'm honest as the day is long. Why is he telling me that he murdered them, and is going to go after their estate? Especially since he knew he was being recorded." She said that she didn't know, but she was looking into it. "I'm going to lose my business, aren't I?"

"No. Once this gets out, that he's done this, then it'll go back to normal. But until then, I think you should have your business closed up, just for now, and go work on your new house." He thought about his home and all the work that was being done on it. "Where are the recordings that you use?"

"I put them in the safe every night. I don't even use them a second time. Ever." She told him that was smart, but she wanted them. "All right. I can do that. Lauren, he killed that couple." He turned in his chair to get into the safe that was under the carpet at his feet.

"Yes, and while they don't know it, I'm afraid that their kids are next." He realized then that Wells had mentioned the children by name and told her. "Yeah, I have a detail on them now. They're with their grandparents for the time being, but there will be more guards around them at all times now. And don't talk to them. I know you want to go there and see them, tell them you had nothing to do with their parents' deaths,

8

but he's more than likely waiting on you to do that. We have to play this very close to the vest."

For the rest of the afternoon he took steps to close his business. Larson knew that it was only temporary—he hoped—but he was still depressed about it. As he called in the service to have them answer the phones, he handed over all the recordings that he had in his safe to Lauren. She said she'd make sure they were safe.

Going to his new home, he watched his dad and grandda as they worked at taking the railing down. It was cast iron, and the previous owners had painted it a bright blue. It was chipped for the most part, but Dad had told him that he could have it looking as good as new in no time. They were going to dip paint it black to match the shutters, the real kind that actually covered the windows. Larson was glad to see something going right.

"You here or going again?" He told Dad what had happened. "Well, I'm thinking that if Lauren says she can fix it, then she can. I got me some helpers in the back yard, tagging what you don't want to pull up. I guess this place had a nice rose garden years back, and they want to come in and mark them for you so you don't pull them up. Said they'd help you make them pretty again."

He headed to the back yard, a place that he was beginning to think was never going to look good or be finished. But the moment he spotted the two women, he began to have hope. In the time they'd been here, not only were ribbons on some of the plants, but there was a large brush pile next to the patio.

"Hello, Larson. My goodness, you have a wonderful place back here. I cannot wait until you put some of these beauties in the next garden show. You'll win for sure." He nodded at Mrs. Frank and told her what he'd found out about the gardens. "She, the missus here, she didn't care much for people. I think her only solace after her son passed was this place. She sure did love to have her roses around. Did you find anything in the house that belonged to her?"

"I'm not sure there was much left. The house had been empty, from what I understand, for a very long time." Mrs. Frank told him to have a look-see in the barns. There was stuff in there. "You think so? I mean, why would it still be here after all this time?"

"She didn't have no one left when she got up there but for a sister that was as mean as the owner was nice. So this sister was some upstart that had it in her head that she was going to live here and carry on being queen of the town. Nobody liked the old biddy, and she only lasted a year, probably less. But she took all the things that were in the house and put them in the barn, last I heard." He watched what she was doing as she continued to talk. "And when I heard that one of you McCulloughs had bought this place, I was tickled pink. You go on now, and you and me, we'll have ourselves a look. Might be some things in there you can use for your place."

They walked to the big barn. It wasn't tall like the one on his brother's place, but it was huge in that it was one level of sprawling wood. He found the light switch just where she said it would be and turned them on. As they lit up, one after the other, he could see that someone had taken care to make sure that nothing was ruined. There must have been a dozen or so cats around. And every one of the boxes was set up on bricks that he was sure matched the ones on the patio just beyond the rose gardens.

"I guess they'll look up to you." She was still laughing as she led him to the back of the barn. She was pointing out that someone had put boxes in this area, and each one of them was marked with what was in it as well as which room it had come from. "Looks like she put everything in here, doesn't it?"

There were over a hundred boxes of varying sizes. There were trunks too…most of them had faded labels on them, but he could make out some of the words. As soon as he realized that there was more in the next stall, he called his mom. She of all people would know what was good to keep or toss out. She said she was in town with the baby but would come by.

"My mom, she's coming to look this over. You think that anything in those trunks will be any good? This one here says it has wedding stuff in it. What do you suppose that is?" Mrs. Frank told him it might be a wedding gown for his new mate when she came along. He didn't comment. Larson was terrified of having a mate.

"She sure did have a good old time with packing this stuff up, don't you think? It might have been easier on her just to leave it in the house. That's my thinking anyway. Well, if you'll be all right here, young man, I'll go back to my garden. I don't mean that it is, but I expect you to invite me out here when it's in bloom. Maybe we can have a garden party when that happens. If you want."

Larson told her that would be fine with him, if the house was finished. She just laughed and walked away. Larson didn't know what she thought was so funny, but he pulled one of the boxes off the shelf and cut the tape. It was old too, probably as old as he was, but when he opened it, he just stared at the contents.

Boxes of seeds were in the box, along with when to plant them and what they were. He picked up the first one of about three dozen and read the label. Basil. He wondered if the seeds were any good after all this time, and opened the box to see them. Inside was a canvas bag of them that had been tied with leather. He discovered that they were all like that as he began to pull a few of them out. He wondered what Mrs. Frank and her ladies' club would think of that.

By the time his mom had shown up, he'd opened three more boxes, each one of them better than the last. And he had so much more to look through. His mom handed him little Samuel and opened some herself. It was going to be fun, just finding out what had been kept for the house.

~~~

"Mom, where are you?" Her mom was her lifesaver, and she grabbed her hand as soon as she was close enough to touch. "I can't do this. I can't believe I ever thought I could. We should leave."

"No. We have things to do here, and you can do this. If it gets to be too much, we'll take a walk. The building is certainly big enough for that. Besides, I'd really like to meet these people. I know that we can't take him home with us, but I'd like to know that he's in good hands." Virginia pointed out that they'd had them investigated. "Yes, but that doesn't mean that they're nice people just because they have money."

They had arrived late last night in this little town. The plane had been delayed twice coming out of California, but that wasn't all. Her luggage had been misplaced, along with a couple of her mom's things. As it stood right now, not only did she not have any clean underwear, but she had nothing to put on her feet but flip flops. And it was too cold for that. The company that owned the airline was sending over a credit card for them to use to buy some things, but she wanted her own stuff. It was why she had bothered packing it after all, damn it.

Her mom tisked at her when she cursed again, then said, "I need to do something. Sitting around here is making

12

me uneasy." Virginia and her mom were to meet with the McCulloughs in an hour. But she had to find a place to get some of her necessities, as well as figure out when they could go home. "How about we hit that little shop there on Main Street? It looks like it might be open for business. I'll buy you lunch."

"All right." The shop had no name as yet, nor did it seem to be a place that showed up on her phone. But it had some lovely displays in the window, and she had already fallen in love with the pretty pitcher and bowl set that sat on a dry sink. "I think I'm going to enjoy having a little getaway here, if only I didn't have to meet any people. And I mean any person. I like my quiet and the fact that no one is around me. But here...I mean, it's so quaint, don't you think?"

It was. The entire main drag was decorated for the upcoming holiday...or what she thought of as a holiday. Thanksgiving was her second favorite time of the year. It was cold enough for a jacket, and the crunch of leaves under her boots made her smile. But here, it looked as if they had gotten a dusting of snow a few hours ago, and then there were the dark clouds overhead.

This little town acted like this was the best thing to ever happen here. There were decorated pumpkins, as well as pretty candles. There were real cornucopias that had small pumpkins in them as well. One shop had brought in a large roll of hay, painted it bright orange, and given it a turkey face with cloth feathers out the back of it. Virginia was making mental notes of it all, just to use in a book sometime.

"Do you suppose that they have any magical creatures about, and this is their way of making sure that things are friendly?" She laughed at her mom's statement. "I know that you don't believe in such things, but I think it's possible. And

13

you certainly write about them enough."

"I like the way I can go into my own little world and make up whatever I want about them. Not being real, that just gives me more to work with. Besides, creatures are around, but not very magical, I think. I mean, who would believe that anyone would be able to do some of the things that are in my books? No one, that's who." She held the door open for an elderly man and woman, and smiled when he tipped his hat at her. "Mom, this is going to be in my next book, somehow, someway."

The antique shop was busy. Two women beside the counter were having a great time talking about some other woman, but in a good-natured sort of way. Virginia supposed conversation with the woman behind the counter had been going on for some time too, from the way they'd gotten comfortable about it. Virginia noticed that in addition to the antiques on display, there were also things like old doorknobs and stained-glass panels.

Virginia wanted it all, from the old silver napkin holders to the beautiful hand-stitched hand towels for the bathroom. She was fingering a beautiful doily when the woman from the counter came to speak to her.

"Beautiful, isn't it? Most of these things were left by a little antique shop that went out of business. The owner of the building bought it, and now I'm helping her sell these things at a more reasonable price." Too much information, she thought, but Virginia told her that was nice. "You're new to the area, aren't you? I'm thinking that you're not from around here."

"No, I'm not. My mom and I are just passing through." Virginia walked away from the display, afraid now. As she went in search of her mom, a woman walked in and started to laugh loudly.

"You should see what Larson has found, Becky. The barn is full of things we can help him out with if he decides he doesn't want all of it." Virginia smiled at her when she told her hello. "On my, but aren't you a beautiful woman? I bet your mother is just as pretty. You have the most gorgeous hair."

Virginia was charmed. Not many people could put her at ease like this woman had, and in only a few seconds at that. She thanked the woman and told her how much she loved the shop. Nodding, she took her back to the display and handed her one of the many treasures on the table.

"That is from the early twenties. I had to look up what it was for. Do you know?" Virginia turned it over and over in her hand, but hadn't any idea. "It's a glove stretcher. I'm supposing that it happens after you wash your gloves that they might shrink, but this might be the oddest thing I've ever had in here. And there are a lot of odd things."

As she showed her around, the other woman pointed out some of her favorites, and other things that she'd had to do some research on. By the time they were at the bowl and pitcher set again, the women still hadn't introduced herself. Virginia met up with her mom just as she was headed to the counter with her own purchases.

"My goodness, Mom. You've bought everything." They were all three laughing when she glanced at the clock above the cash register. "I'm so sorry, but we must go. I have an appointment in a little while. This has been such a pleasure. And if you wouldn't mind wrapping up that display in the window, I'll pay for it now and pick it up later."

"An appointment?" Virginia nodded as she pulled out her credit card. "You're Miss Basil, the author, aren't you? I'm

Bea McCullough. I have a meeting with you as well."

Every part of Virginia wanted to run. She had no idea why, but she had a feeling that she'd been set up. Which was ridiculous. Mrs. McCullough had no idea that she was in town already, much less in her shop, but shaking the feeling had her nervous and scared.

Looking at her mom when she said her name, she felt her mind begin to close down. Her hands were shaking and she felt her breathing start to back up. The pain in her chest was heavy and scary. Just when her vision started to pinpoint, light dancing behind her eyes, she felt the sting of a slap across her face and looked at Mrs. McCullough.

"Are you all right now?" She nodded and started to step away when she felt her feet tangle up. "Hang on now. You need to get your footing right. You scared me. Just take a few deep breaths and you'll be just fine."

"Yes. I have panic attacks now and then." She was seated in a firm but comfortable chair just as a bottle of water was handed to her. "My mom hasn't ever hit me, but that worked. Thank you."

"Like I said, you scared me. I thought you were having a heart attack. Your mom explained that you have panic attacks though." Virginia nodded and sipped the water. "If you don't mind me asking, why? I mean, you came here for this meeting, but you looked like you were being taken to the gallows."

"I'm not good with change and people." Bea sat down across from her and Virginia smiled at her. "In fact, it's caused me quite a few problems with the business I'm in. I don't go to signings anymore because of the way they make me feel."

She was beginning to feel foolish and wanted to leave. But Bea, as she asked her to call her, told her to sit still, her husband was on his way. Nodding, she watched her mom at

16

the counter as she paid for her things.

"I'm sorry you're so nervous around people. My son, Larson, he's like that too. He can handle a few people around him, but not a crowd. I think that's why he works with his computer instead of going out in the public much. He has his brothers do that sort of thing for him." Virginia asked her how many children she had. "Six boys, and now three daughters-in-law as well. My husband and I wanted a little girl so badly, so we kept trying. Then Colin started eating big people food by the time we had our last child, and we decided that we'd be better off with six boys we could feed rather than a pretty little girl to starve."

"There is just my mom and me. She raised me all on her own when my father took a powder." Her mom said she was enough of a handful when she joined them. "Now she and I live together, and she's still taking care of me. When I'm working, I sort of zone out to the rest of the world, and she keeps me cleaned up and fed. And the tea coming."

"I've read a few of your books. What the library has, anyway. And I've only just ordered the new one coming out. I'm excited to read it." Virginia thanked her. "You should come to dinner tonight at our home and we'll skip the meeting, that way you can get to meet my family and we can talk too. I'm to understand that you don't want to meet your cousin. He'll be with the nanny tonight. Too noisy with them all there. Say you'll come over and we'll have a party of it."

"I don't know." Her mom was nodding, so she gave in. "I don't know anything about children, Bea. Not even enough to change a diaper, much less all the other stuff that goes along with them. And as for taking care of him, I can barely take care of myself most of the time. I think he'd be better off with people that want him and will give him a good start in life."

17

"You'll be fine. And don't worry about it, honey. I'll send a car for you around five thirty and you can meet my clan."

Virginia nodded and told her they'd be there. When she was back in her hotel room, she couldn't believe she'd said yes. She needed to get her head examined.

Chapter 2

Larson was ready to call it a day when his dad came out to find him. He invited him to dinner tonight, but all he wanted to do was go home and take a long nap, about three days' worth. But his dad wasn't having it and told him he was going to go. Larson instead showed him the things that he'd found in the barn.

"That is the same little tile that is in the kitchen. I was thinking we'd have to pull them all up and start over, but if you have enough of them, we can just put in new ones to replace the broken ones with these." Larson asked him if someone would be able to tell. "No. The best thing about tile is that it doesn't fade out, but it does break. I loved that old stuff, and I'm surely glad that you can keep it. If you want."

"I do. I've found some other pieces too. I think there are several boxes of the front hall tile too." Dad went and looked at them. "You'd not believe all the stuff we've found. There is some really pretty china in a trunk. And kids' toys that are older than you. And that's not even going through a tenth of what is in here. There is furniture too, some of it I don't have

19

any idea what it might have been used for. I want to use as much of it as we can."

"You find any colored glass?" He told him there were stacks of it there as well. "I can see about having some of those panels we looked at replaced if you want. I'm sure that a couple of the windows have been taken out at one point when they were too broken. It won't be hard to have them matched up to the others, not with the glass that is already here it won't be."

There were trunks of not just china, but everyday wear as well. He'd unearthed some pots too, flower pots that had been put in the corner at some point and forgotten. Obviously someone had spent a great deal of money on them, they were so nice. Some even had dirt still in them. He was telling his dad about the books when he told him about the library that was in the house.

"It's about done. We didn't do much to it other than to make sure that the chimney was all right to use and paint it. The floors were fine too. A little buffing here and there and it'll look good." He nodded, wondering if he could start putting some of this stuff in the house. "What I'd do if I was you, I'd take the boxes in that room and sort them out there. That way if you want, you can spread it out on that table we left in there." He thanked his dad. "The dining room is gonna be the last thing we work on. Gotta wait on the windows to come in, and the pocket doors to that room are being redone. I can't believe that someone actually boarded them over like that. And the expansions that you wanted done, they sure are going to hold a lot of family when it's all said and done. I'm betting your mom will want something like that done at the house too."

"I have to hit the basement. I think there are some boxes

down there too. Mom is going to help me sort things out." Dad nodded but didn't seem to be paying attention. "Dad, what is it?"

"You should go on down there and have a look around while you can. Before we start putting things down there to paint these rooms. I mean, it's a nice place down there. A pretty little kitchen, couple of bedrooms too. And the biggest bathroom I ever seen in an apartment setting. And it's clean too." Larson wondered why he hadn't been told about it. "Well, some people might not like having that sort of space. Might mean someone wants to come and live here and you'd not like it.

"I can see that. But that doesn't sound like something bad. I don't have anyone in mind for that space, but I think it would be nice if one of the others wanted to spend a couple of nights here." His dad agreed with him. "Did you see something down there? I mean, with all this other stuff I have, I don't need any more boxes or such to go through."

"Not as many as we found out in the barn, but there are a few. I'd just store any furniture down there until you decided what you want to keep." He asked him if he thought there would be any mice in the house. "Don't know, but you can bet, if there was one in there, it's packed up and gone now, what with you being a cat. But you come on over to the house tonight. That lady author and her mom—her name is Flo, I think—is going to be there. I don't know why your momma thought it would be good to have her come over like that, but she invited and we're to be there."

"Why?" He told him what mom had told him. "I know just how she feels. I don't care for crowds either. You think she'll be all right with us all? I could stay home and take a nap."

21

"You'll be there or I'll take you to the shed." There wasn't any shed, and his dad had used that threat a great deal over the years. But he did tell him he'd be there. "And don't go fancying yourself up either. Just dinner with the family, like usual."

As he made his way to his apartment, he thought about the house and the treasures that he'd found. Larson wondered what he was going to do with it all when he was finished. He had about as much decorating sense as he did fashion. Neither of them were his strong, nor even poorest, suit when it came to sprucing things up, as Mrs. Frank had said. He'd just have his mom help him out with it. She could take a sow's ear, as dad said all the time, and make it look like a winning prize.

Larson almost hated to go back to his tiny apartment, and was going to ask his dad when he could move into his home. The sooner the better as far as he was concerned. Now that he had been in the place a few times, he didn't want to leave.

After getting a much-needed shower, he dressed in his jeans and a T-shirt. He wasn't entirely sure what his dad had meant about not getting all fancy, but he thought he looked presentable. Getting in his car, he saw two men coming up his drive and knew that he didn't want to be late by talking to them. So instead of waiting for them and whatever they wanted, he drove by them and headed to his mom's. If they wanted to follow him for some reason, he had plenty of family there to back him up.

The drive over was nerve racking to him. He kept expecting a helicopter to come down on top of his car to stop him. His imagination had been running wild since Lauren had left him earlier today, and it wasn't helping his state of mind to have people at his home.

Just as he was pulling into his parents' drive, another car

did as well. This one he knew. It was the family limo. Just as he was getting out, he saw Jon on the porch, as well as Lauren. This could not bode well for anyone. He started for the limo when the cars that had been coming up the driveway at his home were pulling into the drive, both of them with lights on inside the car rather than on the top. Lauren told him to come up on the porch, that the rest of them would help the women. As soon as he was on the steps, the men in the cars got out and pointed guns at them all.

"Christ." He nodded at Colin when he spoke. "She's going to kill them, I just know it. I don't know what department they're from, but you can bet there is going to be hell to pay when this shit is done."

Hawkins and his other brother Parker went to the two women. As they were being escorted up the stairs to the porch, he heard his brothers explaining to them that this wasn't a normal thing for them, to have the police here.

"Hold it right there. Nobody move." Lauren kept walking to them, with Jon right behind her. "I said to halt. I'll shoot you."

"You do and that will be the last fucking thing you ever do. And I won't make it easy on you either. Do you know who the fuck you're waving your Johnson at, dumbass?" He said he was here to arrest one Larson McCullough. "You think you can answer my fucking question? I didn't ask you what you were here for, I asked you if you knew who you were pointing that fucking firearm at."

"Him." That didn't seem to satisfy Lauren, so she told them who she was. The guy paled, then put his gun back at his side. Whoever had told him about Lauren, they'd scared the man enough that he was backing away from her. "They didn't tell us you'd be here, ma'am, nor that he was related to you."

"So, you come into a situation blind and then pull a gun on several people, most of which are related to me, without knowing shit. You fucking moron, what the hell do you think the president is going to say when I tell him?" He asked if she was going to tell him. "Of course I am. Just as soon as you get your ass back in your cars and get the fuck away from here. And if you ever come onto a property again where there are civilians and pull your weapon, I'm going to personally see that it's inserted up your tiny dick so that it'll go off every time you take a piss."

Larson heard his mom sigh and he had to laugh. Getting Lauren to stop cursing had been his mom's greatest failure. Not that she'd admit it, but Lauren did have a way with words. And he secretly thought she was spicing things up a little, just to be pissy. He did so love this woman.

"He was running off when we came to arrest him." She turned to him as the man spoke. "We gave chase and he ended up here."

"I was in my car when they pulled in. I just thought they were turning around. It happens." No, it didn't. He lived too far off the beaten path for that. "As for running off? I had no idea they were coming after me. No one said anything, nor did they have lights or anything else to indicate that they were there for me."

Lauren turned back to the men again. Even from where he was he could see that the man who had done all the talking up until now was embarrassed. And when she asked him if what Larson had said was true, he nodded. Of course, she told him to speak when spoken to.

"Yeah, I can see where he might not have known we was there for him." He looked at him then. "But we're to take him in for questioning. There is some money missing."

"Do you have a warrant? Perhaps something more than someone telling you that you needed to come here?" The paperwork was given to her. "This is bullshit. None of this is even filled out properly. There isn't a name on this. The signature isn't right either. Who gave you this?"

"Mr. Wells. He said that he got it from the station house and that we were to enforce it." Lauren told them that they weren't going to be able to get this to stand up in court if they did that. "I don't know, ma'am. I was told to gather my men, go to get him, and to bring him to the jail."

"You try and take anyone from this family into that mess of a jail, and I will have your head." He nodded and moved back from her. Larson might have laughed if he wasn't trying so hard to look serious. "Get yourself back in that car and get the fuck out of here. And if you try this shit again I'll call my boss, and you know as well as I that he won't suffer fools as nicely as I do."

Larson felt someone staring at him and looked at the woman that had arrived when he had. She was across the porch from him, too far away for him to speak to her, but she continued to stare at him. When he smiled, she seemed to realize what she was doing and her face pinked up nicely, and he smiled bigger. It had been a long time since a woman had looked at him like she had.

The fight between Lauren and the man continued. He was only listening with half an ear. Wells had sent these men to get him. Larson wondered what might have happened to him once they got him to the station. It would be smart of him, he thought, to watch himself, more so than Lauren had suggested. Wells seemed to think that he'd done something wrong, and he wasn't sure that he'd come out on top of this if he was to be caught by the man. Not that he could die, but pain was pain no matter what was now in his body.

"You all right?" He looked at his dad and said that he was. "Them men, they here for that mess up on that poor man Simmons? What's his beef with you?"

"He called my office today, while Lauren was there. He admitted that he'd killed them for the money, and wants me to return the stocks and the money to his account. I don't know what Tom did with the cash—it was a nice sum—but apparently Wells thinks it's all his, and he even admitted to me that he was going to be in the will. Lauren said to watch my back."

"You'd better. I don't know that man, but I did Simmons. Good man, and his wife was in the rose club with your momma. Those kids of his, are they safe?" Larson told him that Lauren was watching out for them. "Then they're as safe as babes in a cradle."

She was staring at him again. While he wasn't sure what was going on, he made his way to her. Even before he was within touching distance, it hit him. Not just her scent, but what she was to him. Mother fuckballs. The stranger was his mate.

~~~

Virginia had never been so embarrassed. To have been caught, not once, but twice, staring at a man? And what a man he was, too. As she had surmised already, he was a McCullough...Bea had told her there were six boys. She had no idea why, but she'd thought that some of them were just that, boys. This man was far from that. And when he made his way to her, his face looking like it had been chiseled from stone, she felt her heart rate pick up and her mouth dry. That had never happened to her before.

26

"Hello." She nodded at him and felt like she was having a stroke. Instead of fainting dead away, as she tended to do when she was having one of these episodes, she put out her hand to hold onto him. "Here, I have you. Let me get you to a seat."

She let him. Another new thing. Men were there for her to observe, not to come to her rescue. Virginia didn't need rescuing, not ever, but she thought she could get used to it if this was…. Where the fuck was her mind going?

"I'm all right." He nodded. "I'm sorry. I don't do well with crowds. And you guys are certainly big. I thought that you'd be boys. I don't know why I thought that when Lauren isn't a little girl, but married to one of you guys. Not you…is it?" She was babbling, and it made her all hot in the face to be caught doing that as well.

"No, I'm not married." He laughed a little. "Are you? Married I mean? It would certainly be my luck if you are."

"What a stupid thing to say to me." She had no idea why, but it hurt her feelings. "If you'd just go about your business, I'll be fine here. Alone."

"I'm sorry. You're not at all what I expected." She wasn't sure what he meant so told him to go away again. "I'm afraid that's not possible now. It seems that we're stuck with each other."

She looked around for some help. Everyone, including her mom, had gone into the house. The cars that the men had come in were gone as well. When she started to stand, he pulled her back to the swing when she was unsteady on her feet.

"I don't know why I'm so lightheaded." He asked her when she'd eaten last. "That could be it. I forget to have a meal at times when I'm writing. If Mom didn't come in and

27

bring me things, I'd probably not eat the entire time I'm in my zone. I have no idea why I just told you that. I'm sure you don't care."

"But I do. I knew you were a writer. Sadly, I've not read any of your books. My mom has. She's an avid reader." She told him her name. "I'm so sorry. I'm Larson. Larson McCullough. I just bought a house that my dad and brothers are helping me with. It's an enormous one too. It needs a lot of work. I'd like for you to come and see it. Also, we unearthed a lot of boxes of stuff that was in the house when the sister of the previous owner took it out to the barn and left it there. Pictures and china. That's what I was doing, looking through it just before I came here."

"Oh, I'd love to see them. Sometimes when I'm writing, I have an idea for things from things that I've collected. Today I bought a lovely pitcher and bowl set to use in one of my books. I have so much better success with being able to touch and handle things." For some reason that made her feel all hot and bothered. She looked at the yard in front of them instead of the smiling handsome face beside her. "I'm not good at being a woman. That's not right. It came out all wrong. It really did sound better in my head, but I'm not like other women."

She was babbling again. Virginia never did that, not even when she was flustered. It was better, she'd always reasoned with herself, to keep her mouth shut. It was much better than just mumbling a bunch of nonsense that no one cared about.

"I should hope you're not like other women." She looked at him, wondering if he was making fun of her. "You're very beautiful. The color of your hair makes me think that it's very curly. Don't all redheads have curly hair?"

"Not all, but yes, mine is very curly. I don't leave it down often. Actually never. The only time it's down is when I'm in the shower. Then it's wet and hangs just straight." She looked away again. "You're making me think and feel things that I don't think are right. You need to move over there or something."

"Do you know much about my kind?" He lifted a small bit of her hair that had come loose from the tight bun she had it in. "You know, shifters?"

He whispered in her ear, making her skin feel all tingly and tight. She wanted him to touch her like that and to go away too. Her body felt like he'd set fire to her, and that, she knew, wasn't a good thing. Clearing her throat, she answered him as best she could.

"Shifter? I don't know what you…. What are you doing to me?" He only grinned and she felt hot. Her body was literally humming with something enigmatic. "I don't know what's going on. I don't even have a clue what I'm feeling."

"It's normal for us." Virginia nodded as his face moved closer to hers. Licking her lips when he was only a breath or two away, she wanted to cry when he paused. "May I kiss you, Virginia? Just a small one for now."

All she could think about was that kiss. His mouth coming to touch hers. And when he brushed his mouth, ever so gently, over hers, she felt as if she had stuck her finger in a live socket while it was plugged in. Then he kissed her.

It wasn't a kiss so much as a devouring. His mouth molded to hers even as his hands pulled her body closer, then she was sitting atop him, her legs on either side of his. When he slid his tongue over hers, she moaned. Virginia wasn't even sure that she could have stopped it. Her body was on fire. Not just fire, but she felt as if her blood was molten lava, and it was racing over her like she'd sat in the sun for hours.

When he pulled his head back, she looked into his eyes.

All she could think about was his beauty. His hunger. And it matched her own. Instead of doing what she normally would have, if being kissed by a near stranger was normal to her, she leaned in and kissed him. Virginia gave him as much as she could, wanting to show him how much he had affected her with his mouth.

Larson touched her. Not just her skin, but her heart and her soul. It was as if she knew him, somehow knew that this was the man for her. And while her logical part told her that wasn't possible, her heart told her logical part to shut the fuck up and enjoy. When he pulled back again, she pouted... another thing that she'd never done before. "We're sitting on the porch at my parents' house where anyone could see us." She told him right now she didn't care. His soft laugh had her smiling. "Yes, well, we'll both be in deep shit with my mom if she comes out here and I'm having sex with her dinner guest on her railing."

Virginia looked at the railing, then back at him when he moaned. "I'm so sorry, but I can't muster up any kind of fear for that." When she slapped her hand over her mouth, she told him that she was sorry again. He pulled her hand away and kissed it. "I don't talk like that. I don't even have sex, or in this case almost sex, with strangers. You must think I'm easy or something. I'm not. I have no idea what is going on with my head today. It's almost as if I've been possessed or something."

He rocked upward and she felt her pussy soak. This wasn't helping, and she told him that. His laughter this time sounded pained, and she leaned her forehead to his. He held her on his lap, but he was no longer touching her the way that he had been.

"We need to go inside. My brothers are telling me that

30

Mom will be out soon." She asked him if he'd heard them shouting out a warning from the house. "Something like that. You didn't answer my question earlier. What do you know of our kind? My mom said you write about shifters like you know them. And while you get most of it right, there are some things that you don't."

"They're make believe." She got off his lap and was distracted by the outline of his cock stretched behind his jeans. "You must be huge."

He laughed and stood up. Virginia couldn't believe the things that were slipping out of her mouth. It was like someone had taken the filter out and was letting her simply say whatever popped into her head. This wasn't her. None of this was.

"I don't know what's come over me. But in answer to your question, I don't know what you mean. I mean, there are no such things as shifters. And certainly no vampires." He said nothing, but she looked up at him. "Right?"

"There are both, I'm afraid. I'm a jaguar. So is my family. A friend of ours is a vampire, I'm sure you'll meet her soon, and her mate is a tiger. Tony the tiger. Also, we have a few others that are our friends. Bear for one, and then there is Jon. You've met him." She nodded, still not sure where he was going with this. "He's everything. I mean, I guess he's not everything, but there are things that he's still not tried yet, so he could be wind and water if he so chose. And you're a human. As is your cousin, Samuel."

"No, that's not right." He nodded just as Jon came out on the porch. She looked at him. He was just a boy, no more than fifteen or sixteen years old. Virginia looked at Larson and let her temper rule her. "What is the meaning of this? Are you making fun of me, for what I write? Let me tell you,

31

buster, I make a great living at writing about that stuff. Stuff that isn't real. There are no vampires. No shifters. And there aren't any brownies, faeries, or whatever else you think to tell me about."

"I'm a cat. A man too, but I can become a cat. Would you like for me to show you?" She shook her head and backed from him. When she hit the railing behind her, she thought that she could run to her car and get out of this madhouse but for leaving her mom behind. "If you run, he's going to take me and chase you. He would love nothing better than to knock you down and leap on you."

"This is wrong. You can't expect me to believe that you're a shifter." Jon said that he could show her. "Show me what? You think you can do this as well?"

"Oh yes." He was standing there one moment, then he was a large hawk the next. Then he was a dragon, a cat, as well as the spitting image of her. When she reached for the railing, suddenly feeling faint, Larson picked her up and told Jon that was enough. Virginia looked up at Larson.

"He's just showing off. Usually he's very laid back, but I think he wanted to impress you somehow. Are you all right?" She nodded. "You're going to pass out on me, aren't you? I have you. I won't let anything happen to you."

When the darkness began to swallow her up—for that was just what it felt like—she let it tumble around her. She heard her mom, then others, speaking, but she was beyond that now. They were insane, her mind told her. *Go to sleep and you'll be fine.*

Of course, she wasn't going to be fine. This man had her, and she wasn't sure how she was going to run off. Because if that part of her stories was true, they were stuck with each other.

Chapter 3

"I think you could have handled this a little better. It's not like everyone knows you can shift into a lot of things." Jon said he was sorry. Again. He was smiling, so Larson didn't believe he was sorry at all. "And I expect you to tell her that you're sorry too. You scared her."

"I only meant to show her that we weren't lying. And so you know, Uncle Larson, she has met shifters before, but not since she was a child. Her mom, never, but she does read her books." He said he was going to have to read a couple of them. "I'd not let her know when you do. I think if she would find out, it would embarrass her more than having her mom tell her that she has."

"What do you mean?" Jon only shrugged as they sat in the bedroom where he'd taken Virginia when she'd fainted. "Are you saying that she's embarrassed by what sort of genre of books she writes? Or just that her mom had read them?"

"Both, I think. It's in her mind that she doesn't want people to think that she does some of the things that are mentioned in her books. They're very erotic." Larson told Jon to not look anymore. "All right. But when she wakes, I'd talk to her. I know that you wish to talk to her, but I mean about your thoughts on her books."

That made absolutely no sense to him, but Jon left him there. He looked at her, laying on what used to be his old bed. Larson then looked around the room. It was hardly noticeable that he'd once been in here.

His mom had asked them all, all of his brothers and him, if she could redecorate the rooms. He hadn't cared. And the things that were in the room when he'd left were nothing that he wanted either. But she had boxed them up and sent them to him, just as she had the rest of them. It wasn't until years later that he opened them, and the memories that had flooded his mind were both nostalgic and funny. He still had the box and the stuff in the back of his closet. Larson wondered if the others did as well.

"What are you doing in here?" Virginia sat up on the bed and looked around. "I guess I'm not at home, am I? Did that guy really shift into all those things?"

"Yes." She sat on the side of the bed but didn't move off it. "Are you okay? I hope you don't mind, but I told them not to wait dinner on us. I told my mom that I'd make sure you were fed, and she said that would be good. Your mom said you missed breakfast and lunch today."

As if it had been waiting for the right moment, her belly growled. She glared at him when he laughed. There was something so adorable about a woman who glared, he supposed.

"I don't know what's going on here. I mean, I have an idea that I've fallen and hit my head, and now I'm hallucinating." He told her that she wasn't. "Can't you just give me a little break here? I'm dealing as best I can. Just, I don't know, lie until I can make up a better story about what just happened here."

"All right, I'm sorry. You were hallucinating." She told him that treating her like a crazy person wasn't helping. "Then how about I sit here and wait for you to ask me a direct question. That way, you can take the information as you can handle it."

"Tell me about yourself. I figure that I should know a little about you since I nearly had sex with you on the porch a little…. How long was I out?" He told her. "That long? I must have needed it. Four hours is a long time for anyone… to not faint." She looked at him like she dared him to tell her that's just what she had done. He wasn't stupid enough to say anything to her.

"Boyd, my brother, is a doctor. He said that you were sleeping for the most part. When he checked you out, he told me that your heart and lungs were fine. However, he thinks you're slightly undernourished, as well as dehydrated." She nodded and told him she'd been told that before. "Mom is having juice made for you, as well as a gallon of her tea. It's good, but no sugar. If you need sugar in it, she said that she'd make you some."

"I don't care for sugar in my tea unless it's hot. This house, it's your parents', I know that I guess. But you guys must have lived here too, right? Is this your room?" He told her that it was, and stretched out his legs in front of him. "I don't want to be a bother here, but do you think I could have something to eat? I don't know what I'm smelling, but it smells like heaven."

"Of course." He stood up when she did, and holding her hand, just to make sure she didn't faint away again, he took her to the hall. "This house has been in my family for generations. It was just a two-room shack when my too many back to remember grandfather built it. Of course, it's been added onto a great deal, and only recently my parents had it redone, inside and out. It wasn't too badly out of date, but the shag carpets were hard to have taken out after all this time."

"It's beautiful, and I love all the old pieces. I'd bet that they're also a part of your long family line. Anyway, you said you had a house but it was huge. By comparison, or just bigger than you had?" Larson told her it was bigger both ways. "I'd love to see it. And the things you found in the barn. I can still go and look, can't I? That doesn't mean that I'm going to do anything with you. It just means I want to see your house and the things that you found. Nothing more."

Larson was saved from answering her when his mom came from the dining room as soon as they were down the long staircase. She hugged them both and told Virginia that her mom had gone with Lauren to see her babies. They'd be returning soon.

"She wants something to eat."

Virginia said she didn't have to go to any trouble. "Whatever you have left over from dinner will be fine. Are there leftovers?"

"Yes, for you both. I saved back some. I have to admit to you, it was hard not to go and get it for your brother when he was begging for more roast. It was by far the best that Reese has ever made." They both followed her into the kitchen, where his brothers were standing around and talking. He knew what they'd been doing…the dishes. It was the way it was whenever they came here to eat. Mom serviced, they cleaned up. His dad was there too, and he was telling the rest of them about his home he'd bought. Mom had yet to see it, but Dad loved it, he thought. She waved a hand at them when

36

she introduced Larson's mate to them. "Boys, I'd like for you to meet Virginia Jacobson…she goes by her author name of J. V. Basil. Virginia, these are my sons."

She was introduced to each of them. They each told her what they did for a living and what order of birth they were. Larson was proud of his family then. First for not overwhelming her, and secondly because no one mentioned that they were mates. He supposed he had Jon to thank for that.

A platter of food was set on the table, and he waited until she was served before he took some too. He was starving all of a sudden, and smiled at his mom when she told him to slow down, there wasn't a fire he had to race off to. The others left them, but Mom sat at the table with them, enjoying a cup of tea and eating a scone.

"I've been thinking about this while you were resting, and I think you might be better telling everyone your name right away. They'll be able to see that you're nothing like that cousin of yours." Virginia told her that she'd not seen either of them for a long time. "That poor girl. Boyd and Mac tried to save her, but the wounds were just too extensive. She told my son Boyd that she was leaving the little boy in his care. We've been keeping an eye on him since he was released from the hospital."

"I hadn't been aware that he'd been hurt." Mom told her that he'd been banged around too, but nothing too serious. "You have to wonder about a person that would do that to his wife and child. I never did like him. And his father wasn't any better. He'd egg him on when we were children. Like it was some sort of game for him."

"Are his parents still alive? I know that they were trying to find next of kin, and didn't have much to go on. This Axel, your cousin, he's sort of a non-entity as far as paperwork goes." She told him that his mom was alive but his dad was dead. "I wonder why Lauren couldn't find her."

"Probably because she'd had enough of them. The two of them together, father and son, were too much for anyone. But she changed her name when Norine caught him with a bunch of child pornography. It was a huge scandal that left her without much. To the town, she died, killed herself, but all she did was change her name and leave the country. I don't think she wants to be found. I think my mom has some contact with her, but you'd have to ask her about it."

Larson made a mental note to let Lauren know that. Virginia pushed her plate away and said she was stuffed. She'd done well, he thought, for someone that hadn't eaten in a while.

"You'll have some pecan rolls, won't you?" Virginia moaned and his cock ached. "I have two left, but you have to eat yours quickly or Larson will take it. He's sort of selfish when it comes to sweets. Not that he eats that many of them, but when there are pecan rolls, he gets in over his head and has a sugar crash a few hours later."

After she ate her roll and most of his, they retired to the living room. He wanted to actually retire with her, but thought he was moving too fast. Mom left them there, saying that she had things to see to for tomorrow.

"She's trying to set us up." He nodded. "Okay, I'm ready for some answers. Not too much detail, if you don't mind, just answers."

"All right. But for each of your questions I answer, you have to answer one of mine." She said that she could do that. "Okay, you go first."

"This thing between us. It's permanent, isn't it? I know

that you told me that your mom said I got most of it right, but that was one of them?" He said that it was. "Yeah, I thought that would be too good if I was wrong about that part."

"You're my mate. I can tell you what that means if you want." She said that would be good. "All right. For my kind, shifters and such, we find one person that completes us. That sounds like a greeting card, I know, but the other person does really do that. My cat is stronger. He's more protective, and he loves you like I do. And that's another thing…we love with all our being, and immediately."

"In my books I say that they bond. I guess maybe it's different with you. To bond with someone, they have sex." Her face turned a pretty pink and he held his humor to himself, not wanting to embarrass her more.

"That's to mate. We have sex to mate. To bond with your mate, you exchange blood. I've not read your books, so I'm only guessing here that you don't have them bite, or that they do something more." She told him that she had only guessed on that part, but no, no one mated like he said. "There are different kinds of shifters. Are you aware of that?"

"No. Just…I'm not sure what you mean." He nodded and got up to go to the books on the shelf. "There are books about this?"

"My mom and dad have written some things up that would be useful to someone that has been turned. You can save someone's life if they're mortally wounded and there is no help for them. But sometimes, because of the trauma that happens when the conversion occurs, they die anyway." He handed her the book. "This might help. But don't take it from here, please. My parents could get into a great deal of trouble for letting something like this get away from them. I think the rest of the women of the family have read it, but to take it away from here would be bad for all of us."

"I'd never do that." She didn't open the book, but looked at him. "I'm terrified, if you want to know the truth. I wrote about them for so long, and now I now find out that they're real. Are there others out there?"

"You mean vampires and such?" She nodded. "Oh yes. We have a good friend, as I mentioned before, that is a vampire. Her name is Victoria. Her mate is a shifter too, but a tiger."

"You mentioned him. Tony the tiger. It took me a moment to realize why that was so familiar to me. I think mostly because I was trying to wrap my head around you being a shifter, but you said there were different kinds. I'm not ready for that right now." He sat beside her. "Your turn."

"How long have you been a writer?" He didn't think she was going to answer, even though it wasn't hard, and a very normal question, but she really had to think about it, he thought. "If you don't want to tell me, I understand."

"It's not that. I have a hard time thinking of myself as a writer. I just do it. I guess it would be better if I told you something else. My mom and I were broke. Broken too, I suppose you could say, but we had nothing. For a while we lived in a car, then when winter came, we moved around a lot. Mostly old buildings that still had windows to keep the cold out. Then someone left a computer in one of the places." He asked her if she still had it. "I do, as a matter of fact, though it's out of date and rarely comes on unless I sweet talk to it, but I have it. How did you know that?"

"You don't strike me as a person that would just toss something out that was important to you." He told her about the boxes of things his mom had given him. "So you see, you and I have that in common as well."

40

~~~

Virginia had never felt this comfortable around someone before. Her mother, she supposed, but not like she did with this man. And it took her a few moments to realize that if she wanted, she could be relaxed around him for the rest of her life. That made her embarrassed again when she thought of waking up beside him every day.

They were headed to his new home. He was telling her about it, the things that he'd found out about it. How it was getting worked on and who was doing it. And the rose garden in the back. She couldn't wait to see it.

As soon as they pulled into the large circular drive, she fell in love with the old mansion. Even with all the large construction containers and equipment lying around, she could see the beauty of the home. He held her hand as they walked up to the house, and she had to stop and just look.

"It's beautiful, isn't it?" She nodded and ran her hand over the stone pillars that would hold the iron trellis that served as the railing for the house. "My dad said we'd have to paint them. I was going to go with black—I figured it would match the shutters—but whatever you think."

"Blue. A very dark blue, and the shutters too." She turned to look at him and saw his smile. "That was very rude, wasn't it?"

"No, it's perfect. The stained glass that is throughout the house has a great deal of blue in it too. So I think that will be perfect." They walked around the entire wraparound porch, and Larson pointed out the things that were being fixed as well as the garden that was in disarray, but she could see what he was talking about. "They tell me that there are a lot of heirloom roses there, as well as an herb garden that was used for the kitchen. I know less about roses than the average

41

person, so I'm happy for the help."

"I bet when they're in full bloom, with the windows open back here, you can smell them throughout the entire house. I bet the colors would be just as bright as their scent too." He smiled at her and squeezed her hand. "I do wax on, don't I? But I can't wait to see them. And the other flowers that are back there."

The barn was just beyond them, hidden behind a group of trees. She wasn't ready for that, wanting to just be with Larson. If she got to pull open just one of the boxes he'd told her about, then she'd be done. That would be all she could think about.

"I have no furniture here. I mean, there are some things in the house. A few things left behind, but nothing much else." She asked him about a bed. "No, no bed. Do I need to add one soon?"

"Yes." She moved away from him, not sure she wanted to see what was written on his face. "I'm not the type of woman that just sleeps with anyone that comes along. I've had sex, and while it was all right, it wasn't all that fulfilling. Do you understand?"

"I do. And as much as I'd like to say it was because you weren't with me, it's probably only about half right. I know that I've been waiting for you forever." He laughed. "That's not quite true. I was terrified to find my mate. I'm very organized. Set in my ways. It's why I love what I do. Numbers never lie to you. And no matter what you do, add or subtract, they still come out with a true answer."

"That thing that happened today, that was because of some of your job?" He told her what had happened. "And this man, this Wells person, he thinks to lay blame of their deaths, as well as the missing money, at your doorstep. That doesn't seem right. I mean, there are laws about that, correct?"

"Yes. He admitted to me that he'd killed them. But as he said, there is little I can do at the moment. Lauren has some pretty good connections, and she's working on that end. I've had to shut down for a few days, just to avoid the press or whatever else he sends my way. I have a service that is fielding calls for me." Virginia asked him if it would hurt him financially. "No, I have more than enough money, even if I have to close up for good, but I don't foresee that happening."

"I had nothing when I started writing, as I said before. It was a way for me to escape the things that were going on around us at the time. When I sent my first story, what I call them, in to a publisher, I fully expected to get back a rejection letter. Imagine my surprise when he sent me a letter asking if I had any more." She laughed a little. "The first thing I got for us was a house. My mom didn't live with me then, but I have since come to depend on her. Housekeepers want to clean up my office. I can't have that happen when I'm in a zone. But I do clean it between each book. Sort of clean slating it, my mom calls it. But she keeps me sane by not bothering me much, and making sure that she slips a meal or two at me daily. And tea. When I am writing, I might drink as many as twenty cups of tea a day."

"I'll remember not to bother you in your office then." She turned and looked at him as he leaned against the house. "I want you. But if you're still not sure, then I can wait. There are hundreds of questions that I can see circling around your eyes."

"Yes. I do have a great many of them. But I want you as well. As I said, sex is all right with me, but don't expect anything earth shattering from me." He laughed and told her she just needed the right man. "I think all men think that."

43

"Come here." She moved toward him and he stood tall. "Christ, you're so beautiful. I cannot wait to have you naked in my arms."

"How does this work?" He started telling her about how a man inserts his penis into a woman, and she smacked him. "I mean without a bed, you idiot."

"Ah. Well, that is a little bit different, but no less fun for us. My cat would like to mark your skin and in turn have you come hard." Her body burned with a fire of need she'd never felt before for a man. "I can smell you. How you're wet for me. How much you want him to do that to you. That would mate you to him, in the event that he has to find you for some reason or another."

"I do. But no sex, right?" He said that was for him. "I want you, Larson. So desperately." He pulled her into his arms and kissed her. It was soft yet hungry, consuming yet tender too. When he lifted his head from hers, she knew then that this man was going to be right for her. That all others before him, and in the future should they part, would be nothing compared to him. "I love you, Larson."

"I love you as well." He picked her up and carried her into the house. She got a brief glimpse of what was going on in this part of the house, and marveled, but only for a moment, at the tall bookshelves that lined the walls. The fireplace that could roast an entire side of beef in it, and the long table that he sat her upon. "I don't know what you think of me shifting, but if you strip down to your lovely bare skin, my cat will show you, in his own way, how much he enjoys having you as our mate by marking your skin."

She stood up and started pulling her clothing off. He stood there, his breathing ragged and his cock hard against the fabric of his jeans. Virginia wanted to ask him if he was

44

going to leave his clothing on or what when he was just gone. In his place was the most beautiful cat she'd ever seen. Not sure what to do, she just waited until she got her fear under control.

"Can you understand me?" The big cat nodded. "Okay, this is odd. Can you, I don't know, talk to me? Wait, I wrote about that once. You have to...I guess you have to taste my blood, right?"

He nodded and pawed at her pants. She wondered if Larson was going to be as impatient as his cat was, and decided that she hoped so. To keep her nerves from getting the best of her, she started to talk. It was that or run screaming from the room.

"I have only a few dressy clothes. Mostly I just wear jogging pants and tees, or sleep pants while I work. And big fuzzy socks. My mom finds them on sale after the holidays, and I have a horde of them." She didn't want to talk about her mom right now, but Virginia thought it was better than talking about how sorry she was going to be after failing him with sex. "I'm not sure what we're going to do about the holidays, but my mom and I go all out with gifts. I think it stems from not having any money for so long. Damn it, I wasn't going to talk about my mom right now."

He licked her thigh and she moaned. Then when he clawed on her skin, she was surprised that it didn't really hurt, but it did bleed a little. Before she could wipe if off, the cat licked it clean and she watched, stupefied, while it healed up without a mark.

I don't want to talk about either of our mothers right now. And if you don't hurry and be naked for him, he's going to tear off your clothing and you'll be naked all the time. She looked at the cat. *Would you like to be naked with me all the time?*

45

"Yes." Larson laughed in her head. "Now what? Do I still strip down or did he want to bite me this time?"

Strip and I'll show you. Virginia barely had her pants and panties completely off when the cat pushed her back on the table. She was just pulling off her bra when he licked her leg, then her calf. Suddenly, Larson was there again. "That's delicious, love. Just what we needed."

Virginia came six times before he finally sat back on his butt and looked at her. She had long since given up on keeping her releases quiet. Screaming each time that he brought her, she knew that she was going to be hoarse in the morning. But it wasn't like she needed her voice to work. When Larson was standing over her again, she wasn't sure that she had any more in her, but the moment he stripped out of his pants and shirt, she felt renewed, her body ready for more. Much more.

He touched his mouth to her with small nips. Each time his teeth grazed over a part of her, she felt her breath hitch, her heartrate double. By the time he got to her breasts, taking each tip into his mouth and suckling, Virginia was aching with the need to come. For him to come inside of her. And when he entered her, it was like she'd been plugged in to something hot and sexy. This was right. This was what making love with a man who loved you felt like.

Larson told her over and over how much he loved her. How he was going to make sure she was safe and happy for the rest of her days. All she wanted him to do was make her his. And when he bared his throat to her, she could see the pounding pulse there, the way his skin and vein twitched, and she wanted to taste him.

Biting him was much harder than she'd thought it would be. And when he cried out, she was sure that she'd hurt him when he told her to come. Blood filled her mouth when she bit down harder, and lights sparkled in her vision. Her body bowed up off the table and she screamed out his name.

"Again," was all it took for her to come the second, then a third time. She nearly begged him to stop when he threw back his head in his own release.

It was spectacular, moving, and sexy. His throat tightened and he cried out, his cat racing over his skin like he had come too. Virginia cried out again when joining him in another release. It was too much, simply too much for her body to handle, and she lost her fight to stay conscious.

Chapter 4

Harley Wells wasn't happy. But then, he rarely was anymore. And now he had some asshole doing things that pissed him off more. Larson McCullough had made his plan to be rich all fucked up when he sold off the shares of Ranger Mountains. They were his shares, damn it, and Tom should have known better than to sell them off. Of course, he was dead now too, but that didn't mean he should have left him hanging around without any money.

They were going to be his life's work, those shares. But now he had nothing to show for all the work he'd done, and the money he'd spent on killing off his partner and changing the will to suit himself. To his thoughts, the children could have the considerable insurance and he'd take the million-dollar shares.

"There is the report you wanted on that McCullough guy. He's as clean as a whistle, by the way." Harley said that everyone had skeletons in their closet, and Dusty said not this guy. Dusty had worked for him since he'd been right out of college, and knew that he didn't have a sense of humor about jobs. "He's clean, I tell you. The entire family is. Even heroes to a lot of the townspeople here about. And his sister-in-law is rumored to have the ear of the president."

"You mean to tell me that he doesn't even have a parking ticket, or even a little scandal from when he was in college? Impossible." Dusty told him to read the report. "He's going to go down, even if I have to make shit up about him."

"I don't think that'll work either, just so you know. I'm telling you, there isn't anyone out there that hasn't had some sort of contact with this family in some way that benefited them. The mother has this charity event that pays for a lot of Christmas for a lot of these kids. Then there's the bookbag drive that they have. Hell, one of the boys, as she calls them, has a pantry in his classroom that helps kids out when it comes to not having enough to eat." Harley asked why someone would do that. "Because they're nice people, I guess."

"You don't believe this shit, do you? About there being nothing on them?" He said that he'd dug deep and there wasn't anything, not even from college. "Well, we'll have to be clever when we make something up, that's all. I want those shares back in the account and the money returned. I've been looking everywhere, and the money that Tom made off the sale is gone. Not even a cashed check for it that I can find."

He'd even gone over Tom's banking statement and couldn't find the money. That's all he wanted, the cash that he knew had to be there for him. He pulled out the paperwork that Dusty had gathered on the McCullough family.

"It says here that they're wealthy. Just how much wealth are you talking about?" He told him. "No fucking way. Why are they even working if they're worth billions? You can bet that I wouldn't be."

"The one that you're talking about, this Larson guy? He

just bought a house. And while he didn't pay cash for it, he could have easily done so without any harm to his lifestyle. He's the richest of the family. And all I can find out about that is that he invests well and shares his knowledge with others so they can be wealthy too." Dusty took something out of the folder. "You might find this interesting. Tom went to him when he wanted to sell the shares in another company that started his company. Larson told him to wait, that it would be making money in no time. In just a short few days, not only did they have the capital to start up this business, but also enough cash flow to keep it running in the black until he went public. The McCullough guy has a knack for buying and selling that no one else does."

He'd been told the same thing by Tom, how the guy could turn a buck into a million. Not quite true, he supposed, but he did make them both a great deal of money. Only in the sense that he had been planning to take it all when his too honest partner was dead. Even the insurance policy that he'd taken out on the couple was null and void now that it was being ruled as a homicide.

"If those idiots hadn't put them in the boat and set them out to sea, I'd be a good deal closer to making myself some cash." He thought of the two men that had suddenly found themselves dead when he'd gone to them to find out what the fuck they'd been thinking. All they'd had to do was kill the couple on board the boat, and then die when he blew up the boat with his own bomb. "All they had to do was go in, fiddle around as seaworthy men, and then, when out to sea, kill them both. Not put them in a raft that would bring them to my doorstep. Fucker shit holes have messed everything up with that stupid move."

"You said you got a call from Tom the night they were

51

killed. Did you ever figure out how that happened?" He didn't want to think of the call he'd gotten, nor the chilling things that had been said to him by Tom. "I hope to Christ no one finds out that he called you, Harley. If they do, they might be able to connect us to the crime. As it is, I'm afraid to answer my fucking door for fear it'll be that moron of a cop they have working here."

Tom had called him at around midnight that night. He was whispering, but Harley hadn't any trouble understanding him. He'd heard gun shots too, during their brief but telling conversation.

"You fucking weed. You hired these guys to kill us?" A gun was fired and, while it sounded to him like it was far away, shattered the quietness of the night as he continued. "You'll never get away with this. I took precautions that will see you hung for this. See if it doesn't. And when you get to the gates of hell, I'll be there waving goodbye to you."

The call was cut off when the sounds of the gun got closer. He laid there in his bed, thinking about how he might have gone about taking these so-called precautions, and decided it was an empty threat. After all this time, someone would have come forward and turned it in, he thought. Still, from time to time, he would worry.

"I want you to find out something on one of the wives. Surely they're not as clean as the men. And you said that one has the ear of the president? Find me a way to make sure that she is as guilty looking as the rest of them. I want this to end." Dusty said he'd be right on it but didn't move. "What is it now, Dusty? Another long tale about how we should just back our bags and get out of town? I'm not doing that. You can if you want, but not me. He owes me."

"You have money, Harley. I do as well. Why don't we just

let this one go and move on? There are too many variables going along with this that are working against us." He might have, if he wasn't so pissed off about the fact that Tom had gotten the better of him. And not only that, all his money was gone. Preparing to be rich had cost him everything. "Please, I'm begging you. Let's just walk away from this one. There might be a bigger fish out there you can catch."

"That stock was mine. And the money I was going to get from the sale of it was going to set me up for the rest of my life. A nice place to live. An island or something. That was seventy-three million dollars, Dusty. That is nothing to just walk away from." Dusty said he'd not realized it was so much. "Yes, and when the government comes to take their share, because they fucking think they can, I'll be long gone, and so will you."

"All right, I'll keep digging, but you have to realize that there's nothing I can do if there is nothing out there. They're the cleanest people I've ever seen." As he made his way to the door, he stopped and turned back. "Harley, if I were you, I'd be thinking of an exit plan. These people aren't ones to fuck with, and they might get you where it counts most."

After Dusty was gone, he looked at the paperwork he'd been given. There was a list of charities that the family not only donated to, but had set up foundations for. He read about the charity that helped families after tragedy struck. Cars were purchased for people who had no way of getting back and forth to work. The father of the clan even helped build and renovate houses for the crippled. It didn't actually say that, but he was reading between the lines now. He hated do-gooders almost as much as he hated the imperfect. Everyone with a dysfunction, in his opinion, should be the ones put in a raft boat and put out to sea. Harley would do it too, if it wasn't too easy to get caught nowadays.

"Fucking humanitarians. Why spend money on people who'd not appreciate it? They're just sucking you dry." Much like, he supposed, he was doing right now. "If you had just kept your nose out of my stocks, then you'd be sitting pretty about now, wouldn't you, Larson, my boy?"

There were more accolades about the McCulloughs. Newspaper articles how they had married and adopted children. Harley didn't believe in taking over someone else's discards. He didn't have any children of his own, not even a wife to share his good fortune with, and he was going to keep it that way. Wives were whiney…they messed with the natural order of things, like not having to share your shit. And children were just nasty little shits that got into everything and broke your nice stuff. He thought he'd rather be handcuffed to a tree for a year than to have to spend an hour with a brat.

The more he read about these fools, the dumber he realized they were. Not only were they rich, but stupid with it too. He calculated that at the rate they were going, they'd be broke in a year at most. But then he found the article that was talking about how long they'd been wealthy. Just as he was closing up the information that made him think that they might know what they were doing, the cop, Joe Windfall, came into his office.

"You find out any more about the death of my partner?" Harley waved off his secretary after she showed Joe in. He'd have to tell her not to just let any Tom, Dick, or Harry in his office like she owned the place. "And his poor children. I bet they're devastated about this. To lose both their parents, and under these kind of circumstances. It must be hard on them."

"It is, but for now they're staying with their grandmother." He'd have to find out where they were and what their daddy might have told them that night. "I've pulled the phone records of both Donna and Tom. And there is a call to you, at a little after midnight on the night we're presuming they were killed."

He'd tried his best to look like he had no idea what he was talking about. And he supposed that now wouldn't be the time to bring up the fact that he thought it was a murder suicide again. That hadn't flown well a couple of days ago, and he doubted that it would now either. Leaning back in his seat, he pretended to think the question over. Like he hadn't thought of that fucking call every day for the last few days.

"Are you sure it was to me? This call? Because I have to tell you, Joe, I don't remember getting one from Tom. Do you suppose he was calling me to warn me or something?" Joe said *or something*, and that pissed him off. He thought if he could, he'd dig up the couple and shoot them himself this time.

They'd been shot once in the head. And there were defensive wounds on them both, he'd been told. Then there was the added fact that they'd been found adrift in the ocean without food or water, and no gun. He hated everyone right now. Then he looked at the cop in front of him and had to think of an answer.

"What night was that? It's all blurring together now. I don't remember a call from him, as I said, but then I've had phone issues before." He asked him what sort of issues, and since he'd never had any, he didn't know what to tell him. Instead, he changed the subject. "The people that were on the boat with them...have you found out who they were?"

"We know that the Simmonses had hired a crew to work with them and to show them the ropes, so to speak. They were to supply them with the food they'd need, cook, and help them learn to sail their boat so they could go out on their own with the children the following summer. So far, all we've been able to find is that you recommended them." He asked him how he'd come to that conclusion. "We have a note, in Tom's handwriting, which tells us that."

"Really?" He wanted desperately to ask him if there was anything else, like where the fucking money was now, but didn't. This was getting worse and worse all the time, he thought. "I might have mentioned something like he should find someone to help him out, but I don't remember telling him who to use."

The copy of a sheet of paper that slid across his desk was indeed in Tom's girly handwriting. And it did say just what the cop told him. That he had recommended a firm by the name Boating Made Easy, with not only a phone number, but that he'd given them a five-star rating.

"The thing is, we can't find anything about them. This company, I mean. We know that he called them…he wrote that down, as well as the names of the crew members, where he was to meet them when they took off, as well as another phone number. Both of which are no longer working." He handed him a copy of the next note. "Tom called them, and talked to them off and on over several days. And he wrote notes about the conversation on each call. That's how we found out that he'd called you. We pulled his records, as well as bank and security cameras on his home and here. Things aren't as cut and dry as you'd like us to believe, Harley. Did you have anything to do with the deaths of your partner and his wife?"

Harley wanted to squirm. He wanted to order the man out of his office and tell him to leave him alone. The office he was in was hotter than it had ever been. Stuffy too, as he felt sweat running down his backbone like a fucking waterfall. This wasn't good. Not even a little bit good. As he looked at the notes, he noticed that his hands were shaking a little and put it down. Christ, he was looking more and more guilty all the time.

"What a question to ask me about Tom and his wife. Of course I didn't. But I just don't know how I can help you with any of this. I guess, as you say, I did give him the name of the company he used, but I can honestly say I don't remember. It might have been something I said off the cuff to him. We were good friends, and I miss him terribly." Joe nodded, but didn't say anything. And unlike his normal self, Harley felt the need to fill the silence. "I can go over my notes at home and see what I can find if that helps you."

"Sure, we'd like that. And we've a warrant to take his computer to the offices. I told my boss that I didn't think I'd need it, that you'd cooperate more than anyone would, but he insisted." He saw men in the outer office putting things in the box now, and his secretary helping them out by pointing at other items of interest. "You don't care, do you, Harley?"

He did. Very much so. He'd not been able to get into his computer since it had a password on it. And he'd tried about every combination he could until it locked up. This wasn't going anywhere near the way he needed it to go. Harley actually considered just getting up and leaving the office, then the state. As surely as he was sitting there, he knew they were only steps away from arresting him.

"Well, I just wanted to keep you updated on things and to get his computer. If you remember anything, Harley, I'd surely appreciate you letting me know. This has been a hard case for us all, you included, I bet. To have such a nice man go like this." Harley said he missed him every day. "I bet you do.

He always said that you were a good partner to have."

As soon as the cop left, Harley got up and closed his door and locked it. Going back to his desk, he laid his head down to try and calm himself. Christ, this was something that he'd never had to deal with before, and he was sure he was going to end up with a heart attack if he had to sit through another visit from the cops. Deciding to go home for the day, he packed up his things, including the notes, and noticed that his file on the McCulloughs was missing.

"Mother fucking bastard took it." He wasn't sure if it had been the cop or Dusty, but this shit was getting old fast. He needed a break in this thing so he could leave the country. "I'm too old for this shit."

He left his office just as the police were going through Tom's office. He'd have moved into it by now, but there were things that he had in his office that Tom didn't. Like a safe that was hidden away, as well as other items, such as guns and his books. Damn it all to hell, he thought, he should have killed him here and been done with it.

~~~

Virginia was working when someone knocked on the door. She didn't want to get up to answer it, and had even decided that she was going to get her a sign that said for people to go away or hire someone to do that for her. She hated interruptions. When the doorbell rang three times in a row, she got up and stomped all the way to the front hallway. She was both annoyed and surprised to see Rich and Bea there, and the bundle they had in their hands.

"We have to go on a trip. Not an emergency, not really, but we have to go." She nodded at Bea. "Everything you need is in that bag. He's been fed, and should take a long nap for you. But we have to go."

Before she could say a single word, even if she had been able to think of anything to say, they were in their car and gone. That was when the bundle in her arms started to cry. It was a baby. And she'd bet anything that it was her cousin's.

Taking it into the house, kicking the bag that had been dropped off too, she pulled some of the blankets off his face and looked at him. He'd stopped crying, but now he was looking at her as if he were studying her for any defects. She did the same to him.

"Well, thankfully you look like your mother and not that asshole of a dad." He seemed to agree with her and yawned. "Yes, well, I do hope you take a long nap, kiddo. I don't have the time or the energy to mess around with you today. And I doubt very much anyone would have left you with me if they knew I don't even know how to change a diaper."

He yawned again and she joined him this time. Sam was a cutie, she'd give him that, with his pursed lips and tiny little nose. She wanted to touch him, and actually looked around to see if anyone would see her. Then she ran her fingers over his soft cheek, and that made him yawn again.

"You can't keep doing that, you know. If you do, then we're neither one going to get shit done today." She figured that she should have cleaned up her language, but decided that if he was going to be hanging around her for any length of time, he'd better get used to it. "I'm not changing my ways for anyone, kid. Just so you know to keep that in mind as we deal with this. And I don't think for one second that whatever they're doing, it would have been a bother to take you with them. I'm thinking, and I'm more than likely right, that they wanted me to see you, and here you are. They're sneaky, those parents of Larson."

Taking him into her makeshift office, she thought about

what it was going to be like having him around. She'd thought about going to see him over the last couple of days. And since she was pretty much going to be living in the same town as him, she might as well get used to the little boy. She thought about the McCulloughs and their little plot to bring them together.

"I don't think anyone in their right mind would think that you being here with me without supervision would be a good idea, do you? One of us is going to get hurt in this, and I'm betting that it's not you." He just stared at her, his eyes blinking slower all the time. "I think they just wanted to see if you and I could get along. Do you think we can?"

After unwrapping the blankets off him, she laid him on the couch that had been delivered this morning. It was nice and soft, and she'd wanted it for her office. Of course, Larson had told her to take it. He now wanted something bigger for the living room. The room that she'd been working in had been the living room, and she thought he was nuts for wanting something bigger. But then she thought of the size of his family.

"You're small, aren't you? I mean, I didn't expect you to be toddler sized, but you're tiny." He closed his eyes, and she watched his little lips move like he was sucking on a bottle. "There are things about you that annoy me. Like how cute you are, and how you've already wormed your way into my heart. Darned McCulloughs. They knew just what the heck they were doing, didn't they? Well, I don't think we should tell them that, do you? They're going to think they're the greatest matchmakers in the world if we do."

Virginia didn't get up and go back to her computer. The baby just laid there, his arms stretched out over his little head like he had not a care in the world. His little shoes, no bigger than the palm of her hand, were ridiculously adorable, and she found herself checking his little pockets on his pants and wondering why he'd even have them. It wasn't like he had keys or a wallet to put in them. But then she giggled, just thinking of the tiny little wallet he'd have with miniature little pictures in it.

She couldn't just leave him there. What if he needed her? Then there was the added problem of him rolling off the couch. She'd hate for him to be hurt while she was with him, so when he seemed about as asleep as he could get, she put him on the floor with his blankets. While that might have been better, it wasn't foolproof. What if someone stepped on him? Or he got hit by something that fell off her desk?

She spent a good hour just watching him, making sure that he didn't roll over or have anything fall on him. Virginia looked up the care for infants, and found that not only did they not roll over on their own at his age, but that they pretty much slept all the time when left alone. She wasn't sure that was right, so she was looking at other websites for babies when Larson joined her.

"Your parents are sneaky." He laughed and asked her why. Pointing to the baby on the floor, she continued. "They just up and left him here. I don't know anything about kids, and less about them at this size. He's really small, isn't he?"

"No, he's about normal, I'd say." She nodded, remembering that he had brothers with kids. "You must be doing something right. Mom said that she has to hold him all the time when he's sleeping so she can let him rest. I've yet to see him just lying down like this."

Virginia smiled. It felt good to be able to do something better than Bea. The woman was a wizard. She watched the little boy who was related to her, and wondered what sort of man he'd be. Like his father? His mother, perhaps? She knew next to nothing about Norine other than that she was stupid, she thought, for staying with such a man as her cousin. Looking up at Larson, she put the question to him.

"I mean, will he be a drug addict, you suppose? Or perhaps beat his wife or other women?" He leaned back on the couch and asked her what she thought. "I don't know, honestly. I suppose that he'd only do what he saw, and if he's adopted by parents that do the same as Axel, then yes, I would think he would."

"However, he might end up with people that only have him to fulfill a need of some sort. You know, pressured to have a kid. They might not change their lifestyle. It might not be abusive in the physical sense, but it could be just as bad if they have no time for him." Virginia glanced down at Sam and saw that he was looking at her. "He will be in good hands should you and I adopt him."

"I didn't think I'd want a child. Not just not Axel's, but any child. Then you came into my life, and it's all I can think about lately. You know, having a child with you." She looked at Larson. "I would like to make sure that he is loved and cared for. I want him to feel love and know that he's loved too. But I want children of yours as well. Not that I'd treat Sam any differently, but to carry your baby would be the best feeling, I think."

"I love you, Virginia." He leaned down to kiss her just as someone cleared their throat. "Go away, Dad."

"I can't do that, son. The police are here." Larson stood up and she did as well, standing over little Sam to protect him. "They said that they have a few question to put to you about that man's death. Said that you weren't in any trouble, but that he just needed questions answered. I don't know. He looks powerfully upset if you ask me. Your brother is on his way, and he said for you not to say anything."

"All right. What did they say they were here to do?" His dad said just questions, for now. "Dad, I didn't have anything to do with their deaths. I liked Tom and Donna."

"I know that, boy. What you think I'd think? That you'd gone out on their boat and shot them up? No, I don't think that. Now you're to sit in the kitchen and wait for Colin. He said that he's got someone to help you out."

"Lauren?" His dad said he didn't know. "She'll shoot now and never ask questions. I don't know if you know that or not, but she's sort of protective of us all."

"I know that. Boy oh boy, do I know that."

He was laughing as he left the room. Virginia decided that she loved that old man more than she did anyone she'd met of late. About as much as Larson, but in a different sort of way.

Chapter 5

Larson waited for his brother. He figured that if Lauren showed up, this would be over before it began. She would kick the cop's ass all over the house then ask him, maybe, why he was there. But as soon as Colin and the president stepped through his back door, he stood up and so did Joe. Virginia came in with the baby in her arms, and he knew that she was going to blast the president again.

Just two days ago, he'd shown up to talk to him, but he'd encountered Virginia first. Lucky for the men with him, Larson had told them to back off or there might have been a major fuck up. Larson would have killed them both. But Virginia had given him the business, and Larson would have thought Jarvis would have learned by now not to show up unannounced.

"I thought we talked about this?" Jarvis told her that he was sorry, but this was an emergency. "Yes, I understand that, but you couldn't have picked up the phone? Sort of warned me? What would you have done had I been in my nightgown? Or something equally embarrassing?"

"I would have told you how lovely you look, and then kissed you on the cheek. Just as I'm about to do." He did kiss her, and then fussed over the baby. "He looks like you, Larson. I think he'll blend well into this family. And Virginia, I am profoundly sorry for your loss."

She nodded at him and started for the door. He knew that she was working on a deadline, and asked her if he could take Sam. Virginia assured him that she was fine and left them. He looked at Joe when he laughed.

"I would hate to be on her bad side. She has a way about her that just screams 'Don't fuck with me.'" Dad hit Joe on the back of the head and then laughed. "Yes sir, she's a tricky one, that woman is. But as to why I'm here. I wanted to make you aware of a few things, and to let you know that you're no longer a suspect in the murders of Tom and Donna."

"I was one?" Joe said only in the sense that he'd made a great deal of money from the sale of the shares. "Yes, but I told him that he should wait. And I have no idea what he did with the money either. I did it just like I do for every client I have."

"Harley Wells ask you about it?" Larson told him what had happened, and then told him that he had turned over all the records to Lauren. "I know that. Christ, this man is so guilty that it's looking like he might have had a hand in the murders of the two men we've been looking for too."

"What men?" Joe told Jarvis who they were. "You think that he killed the men who were actually responsible for the murders? Why would he do that, other than he's a murderer? I mean, you must have a theory, correct? If so, I'd like to hear it, young man. I've not had a good day as yet, and you might just be the one to take me out of the crapper."

"I do...I did, I mean. I thought that they were to kill the

66

couple and let the ship blow around them. Or, and this one is my wife's theory, that the men were to kill them and the bomb was put in there to take care of the killers too. It was put there by Wells to get rid of any witnesses and to clean up the deaths. I'm beginning to think she's right on hers." Larson thought so too, but waited on Joe to continue. "We know that the men were paid by someone, and we're reasonably sure it was Harley. But what he doesn't know, and few do other than a trusted couple of people, is that the killers left a note on Tom. In his wallet. It was detailed into what they were told to do, how much they were paid, as well as that they thought they were to die too. But, and this is the real kicker, they didn't mention names. I don't know if that's because they didn't know who paid them, or they were afraid of him finding out they'd let the cat out of the bag."

"So what is it you need from me?" Joe handed Larson a little device. "I don't know what this is. I'm sure I should know, but I can't think beyond the fact that Harley has killed several people, and has no qualms about continuing what he's done for money. Because sure as I'm sitting here, that's what it was for. All he talked about was the shares and the money that he said belonged to him. And—this one scared me more than the other things he said—that he was going to be in the will. Christ, the man has balls, I'll say that for him."

"It was. The money that you sent to Tom, how did you send it?" Larson told him that he had the money deposited into an account, then had a cashier's check written to Tom from that account. After that a courier sent it to him. All in one day. "That money, how much was it?"

"Just over seventy-three million, minus my cut of ten percent." He nodded. "I don't understand what you're getting at here, and I'm sure you are getting at something, but right

67

now, I can't think."

"The money is gone...or I guess, unaccounted for. It never showed up in his personal or business account. As far as we can tell, the money didn't go anywhere after he signed for the courier receipt the day before he left." Larson asked why that was important. "That's what this is going to tell us. We bugged Harley's office. And I need your help to tell me the voices that you hear. We know his, but not anyone else that might be coming and going there."

"I might not either." Joe said he was aware of that, but any help he could give him would be more than they had before. "You think he has a partner in this?"

"I do. Even if he did all the killings himself, which I'm not saying that he has, there has to be someone that he trusts more than he does anyone else. He'd need someone to cover for him if there are questions. To find him guns and to help him get the bomb on the boat. We know that the men who killed the Simmonses didn't go up with the boat, but they have been killed by someone. Also, there are people going in and out of the building now that while we might know them, we don't know what sort of ties they might have with Harley. Too, someone has tried to get into Tom's work computer and it shut them out. We have a few people working on that now." He looked over at Jarvis. "Lauren is good, by the way."

"She is at that. And if she can't figure it out, then no one can." Larson believed that too. Jarvis laughed as he continued. "She's already broken the lock, hasn't she?"

"Yes, just this morning, and you'd not believe some of the crap we've found on it. Tom was suspicious of Harley for a while now. I don't think he thought he was going to kill them, but there is money missing from some of the business accounts, as well as some unexplained money being moved around. I think Tom found Harley's stash, and took it to put back into the accounts that Wells took it from. Not legally, but he was only returning it to the accounts so as not to have a red column in his business. Tom was a very smart businessman."

"Wells is claiming that I took the money, and that I had the Simmonses killed just to get all of it. I don't work like that." Joe said he knew that. "None of this makes any sense, you know that, don't you? I mean, why would he think that ruining my business and calling me a thief is going to get him anything?"

"Because if he focuses all this onto your plate, he's cleared of anything else. Or so he thinks. He has gone about his business like nothing is out of the ordinary. He can look for the money and when he finds it, if he does, then he'll skip town. Or more than likely the country. But there isn't any money for him to fall back on right now. By this afternoon, he's going to be notified that not just all the accounts for the company are closed up, but so are his personal ones. Just to keep him in town. And we've also had someone put a hold on his passport, just in case he gets something from someone and tries to leave without us knowing."

Jarvis stayed after Joe left him the device and instructions on how to use it. He was going to be notified by someone in the station when there was activity at the offices. All he had to do was listen to it and call them back if he knew who a person was. The station was also recording everything in the event that he might miss something.

"I've come to talk to you as well. After talking things over with Lauren, I've decided that I need you for a couple of personal things." Larson said he'd do anything for him. "I need someone to invest my own personal money. I have a lot, for me anyway, but I'd like to have enough that I don't have to live where the government tells me to when I'm no longer president."

"You think anyone is going to let you not take the next term?" They both laughed, but Larson was serious. He was a good president and the people knew it. "I can do that for you, but as I'm pretty sure you know, I don't charge family my cut...and you are family, by the way."

"I have to insist that you do for me, just so that there is no one coming back on either of us. If it gets out that you didn't take your cut, which I believe to be too small, then there will be hell to pay for both of us. As I think Lauren has mentioned to you, people do like a scandal, and that would be ripe with it for them." Larson guessed he was right, but he didn't like it. "Also, I'm to understand that you have a realtor's license. I'd like for you to purchase me two homes. I have the details on them, and then leave them in your name for the time being. I don't want people to speculate where I might be going when I leave office."

"I can do that. I've done it before when a company or person wants to purchase a few acres or a business, but doesn't want anyone to know who the buyer is until they start construction. But you'll be responsible for any taxes or liens." Jarvis said he could do that. "All right then, you just tell me where they are and I'll do that for you. Anything else?"

"Yes, it's about your wife. I'd very much like it if the two of you were to come to the White House and be my guests. Nothing going on, just a dinner where we can have a nice meal."

"At the White House? Like it's nothing but a few people having a beer and a pizza?" Jarvis said they could have pizza if he wanted, but he was thinking something more substantial. "You know that Virginia is going to have a kitten, don't you?"

"Yes, that's the fun in this. Also, when will she be having a kitten? I'm sure that you've talked about it. And you are going to raise young Samuel, correct?" He said he didn't know at this point, but he thought so. "Good. Also, and this is just between the two of us, and your mate, I suppose, I'm not running for next term. I've decided that I'd like to be my own man for a while. And the things that went on with my predecessor made me realize that I don't much care for politics. They're too much. Of everything."

"I'm sorry to hear that." Jarvis stood up and said he had to get back. "It will be nice to have you around more, I suppose, without all the guards and such. I know that you'll still have the security with you, but you wouldn't have to sneak around like you do."

"Yes, there is that as well. I want to travel. On my own time. I would like to read a book that has nothing to do with politics and such. It doesn't mean that I'm going to bow out of it completely, but I would like a sort of rest, you might call it." He laughed a little, and Larson thought it sounded so sad. "I want a life like the rest of you have. I don't get that much where I am now."

After he left, Larson went in search of Virginia. He just needed to be with her, to hold her too if he could. The writing cave, as she called it, wasn't nearly finished, but she was working away when he went in. The baby was asleep on her chest and snoring a little. She turned to smile at him.

"I love this. I could do this, I think. I'm not naive enough to think that he's going to be this easy all the time, but I'd like to adopt him." Larson said he wanted to as well. "Also, please get my room done soon. I really need my own space, and this isn't it."

He laughed when he sat down on the couch that had been

brought in, and looked around. It was a mess. Whenever they had to bring something into the house, be it wire or tile, it had been put in this room. Larson told her that if she could work for a couple of days in another part of the house, he'd put it on the priority list.

"Yes, I can work that way for now. But I need my own space. And my things from home too. Also, I wanted to talk to you about my mom. I need her here too." He said that he thought that she was going to live with them. "You'd not mind? I mean, she isn't any trouble. I know that she's been staying at the hotel and all, and I'm afraid that she'll think I don't want her here, but I need her."

"Of course you do. Why don't you have her come by sometime today, and then we'll let her pick out what room she wants. We might as well have it done the way she wants, don't you think? Or, and I just thought of this, there is an entire living space in the basement. It also has its own entrance, so she doesn't have to come through the house to go to her space." Virginia nodded, and he could see tears in her eyes. "Don't cry, love. I can't stand to see a woman cry, and your tears would be the hardest to deal with."

"You're the very best. Did you know that?" He said that she had to say that around his mom. "I will. By the way, she called here a few minutes ago, telling me that they'd had nothing to do but wanted me to see Sam. I told her that I could forgive her if she would be his grandma and not his sitter. She seemed to think that was a good trade off."

"Great. Now, I must get to working on a few things in the other part of the house. If you need me, you know how to get in touch with me." She said that she did. "Also, Dad told me that he was bringing us over some of Sam's things, and a baby bed for him. I think we'll put him in our room today, and have his room done over the next few days as well."

"All right." She turned back to her computer, then looked at him. "I love you, Larson. Thank you so much for being so understanding and wonderful to me."

"I love you as well."

He left her there, with Sam sleeping on her chest and her fingers racing over the keys. He was loving domestic life a lot more than he'd thought he would. Finding his dad working in the kitchen, he explained to him what he needed. In less than an hour they had Virginia set up in the dining room and a crew in her office moving things around. It was going to be a long day, and he loved it.

~~~

Harley hung up the phone and stared at the envelope in front of him. It had arrived over an hour ago, and he wasn't sure what was going on any more than when he'd opened it up. His accounts had been seized. He looked at Dusty when he came into his office.

"I can't get to my money." Dusty asked him why not. "The bank said that the federal government came in and told them that they were to put a lock on my accounts, as well as all my credit cards. I couldn't get a dime out of the bank, and I'm pretty sure that I couldn't pay for a newspaper with my cards now. And they won't tell me what's going on, nor why they did it. I'm thinking that it's that fucking McCullough person doing this. You said that his sister-in-law had the ear of the president, didn't you?"

"Did they tell you how long it would be before they let you have access to them?" He said he'd been trying to figure that out. "I don't understand. Don't they have to give you fair warning or something, so you can get some ready cash out while they figure it out?"

73

"Apparently not. I think that's the plan when they do this. To catch you while you're down. I swear to Christ, this is getting more and more fucked up every day. I need to get this shit finished so that I can skip town." Dusty reminded him that he'd told him to do that a few days ago. "Well, aren't you just the smartest man in the room? I told you, this is seventy million dollars. I can't just walk away from it. I have things I want to do. And you'll love this, but I don't have any money anywhere. I just called my dealer that I have my overseas accounts with, and they said that my accounts have been empty since the day that Tom left. He fucking took it from me, I just know it."

"You mean he stole the money that you stole from him?" Harley glared at Dusty. "Well, you have to admit that it is sort of funny. I mean, he wasn't nearly as stupid as you thought he was. The man has balls, or had them I suppose. He really reamed you over. Have you had any luck finding the kids? I'm sure that they might know a thing or two about what Daddy and Mommy were up to when this shit happened. Not to mention, right now, it might be our only way of making any kind of money out of this deal."

"No. I'm thinking that someone has them under lock and key so that I can't find them. I'm telling you right now, Dusty, that when this shit is done, I'm going to find Tom's grave and piss on him. Even from the grave, the man is fucking me over." He looked at his notes he'd been taking since he'd come in that morning. "Also, McCullough has closed up his offices. The only information that I have on that is through his service. I can't even call his home. There is no listing for it. And when I tried to leave a message with him to call me back, the person on the phone said that Mr. McCullough won't be taking any calls that aren't deemed emergencies. Apparently, she thinks me wanting to talk to him isn't considered an emergency. Fucking bitch."

"He's working on his house now, him and a large crew. I just drove by there. He's got a couple of different crews crawling all over the place. I think he's even putting in some extra security around the homestead as well. Like he doesn't trust anyone." They both laughed. "Anyway, I was going to go by there anyway, but if you want, I can go there and muss things up for him a little. You know, piss him off. Just let me know."

"You do that. Go and set fire to a little bit of it. I would imagine that there are all kinds of flammable things in that place. Might even have a marshmallow or two while it burns out of control." Harley liked that a lot, but he also knew that Dusty wouldn't do it. He hated fire and anything to do with it. If someone had a fireplace running in their home, he'd not go there. He had a real phobia. But they did like to pretend that he'd do it. "Also, there are a couple of places downtown that I think his family might be owning. Might do us some good to get them all riled up too. I don't know why, but I hate how calm they are about everything, and so goody-two-shoes about what they do to help out the stinking poor and underprivileged. I want them to fucking help me. Do you think they will? Hell no, not even enough to call me back."

"I can do that, no problem. But as for calling you back, you're on your own with that one. I'd say avoid them, but that's just me." Dusty didn't leave. But it mattered little to Harley. They weren't best friends, but they were friendly. And Dusty had been working with him since they'd been boys together in the orphanage. "I have some money, Harley. If you need cash, I can get it for you. They don't know who I am, so that'll work in our favor for the time being."

"I would like that, thanks." Dusty told him that he'd get it for him when he left. "Thanks. I need a few things around here too. You know that when that cook left here, he must have taken everything with him. The cupboards are bare. He even took some of my best wines with him. When I find that sucker, I'm going to take it out of his hide for what he did to me. That just ain't right."

"No problem." Dusty stood up then, and Harley leaned back in his chair. "You're not going to leave, are you? You're going to get yourself caught up in this and end up in jail, Harley."

"I'm not going anywhere until I have that money. Someone somewhere has to know where it is. And when I get it, I'll be gone so fast that I won't even leave a trail to find me." Or at least he hoped so. "Thanks for the loan, Dusty. I appreciate it."

After Dusty left him, Harley started looking over his plans. He'd been revising them for the last several days because every time something got moved in his way or someone would come up with something more, he'd have to make adjustments. It had been simple at first, before Tom had ended up dead, but nothing was so simple any more.

The shares were something that he'd been looking into to buy on his own. But really, he didn't have the cash nor the knowhow to buy them. So, when Tom had told him, several days later, that he'd bought the shares, he'd asked him how much he'd had to spend.

"I have a broker. And while I really didn't have the ready cash money, it was easy to get a loan on my car and then use the other shares that I had for something else." He asked him why he'd do such a thing. "My broker. I'm telling you, Harley, the man is a wizard at making money. How do you think I got the capital to buy this place? He turned me into a millionaire overnight. And I bought and sold when he told me. Now, as it stands at this moment, I'm about double what I paid for the stock. And it's only been a few weeks."

So, in an effort to see just how good this broker was, Harley began to watch the stock, and it did indeed go up. Once, right before Tom sold it all, it dipped down a little, but not that much. And his ten-thousand-dollar investment had turned into millions. And that was when Harley had hatched a plan to take it from Tom and to rid himself of the dead weight that his partner was. Harley wanted to be rich, of course, he just didn't want to have to figure out how to do it when the man in the same building as him had more than enough for him.

The plan to kill Tom off had come to him one night while he'd been watching the news. Some kid had killed off his grandda for some coins that he had and the kid wanted. He'd been such a fuck up since the beginning of the whole thing, and had been caught within hours.

But Harley had made notes on other murders that he'd found on the Internet. The things that had tripped others up, and who had told on them. He even looked around for ways to murder someone to figure things out, and ways that had worked the best. He hadn't gone that far...he didn't need to when Tom bought the used boat and he'd had an idea.

Every one of the murders, however, said that it was the change in their lifestyle that had eventually given them away. That spending money that was coming, paying people when the deed was done, was the surest way to get caught. So, he'd taken care of that beforehand. Then Tom and his wife had bought them a boat. Something that seemed to be the best way to get rid of a nosy partner had been the perfect thing for him.

He'd been a model of a broke man before he'd had Tom killed, and since then too. That's what made the fact that Tom had taken the money out of his accounts so aggravating. Harley really was broke, and now his accounts here were closed to him as well.

Things were going to have to break soon or he'd be in prison. Not for the murders that he'd committed, but because heads were going to roll if he didn't have something go his way soon. Every move forward he thought he was making, it was actually two steps back. It seemed that every time he could see the light at the end of the tunnel, someone would snuff the fucker out and he'd be in the dark again. That fucking McCullough prick was the beginning to the end of this shit, and he had to make him pay. He wasn't sure how yet, but he would.

When Dusty returned an hour later, Harley knew he was upset. He just sat down in the chair and didn't speak for several minutes. The way he was looking, sort of murderous, Harley thought that the person who would have messed with this man was going to be dead very shortly. When he spoke to him, Harley could hear the controlled anger in his voice.

"Did you tell anyone that we were working on this?" He asked him why he thought that. "Because my accounts have been seized as well. Not only that, but my car has been impounded, as well as my locker that I have my things stored in. My guns, Harley. All my guns and ammo have been taken by the fucking government. I don't even vote, so how the fuck else would they have found me?"

"I don't know. I really don't. I haven't said a single word to anyone about anything between us." Dusty got up to pace, and that was when Harley noticed the gun in his pocket. "You come here to kill me, Dusty? I hope you're only carrying so that you can protect yourself. We've been through a great deal together, and I would surely hate to have to kill you over something I had nothing to do with."

"I don't have a pot to piss in right now, Harley, so don't go whining to me about how we've been so tight. You'd turn me over to the Feds in a heartbeat if it would get you out of going to prison. We both know that. I'd do the same to you. But this is bad. Really bad." He asked him how not having his cash was going to hurt him so badly. "The guns, you moron. They'll be able to solve a great many cases with just running a few tests on them. And there are notes where bodies are hidden. And before you tell me how stupid that was, you should know that you're mentioned in there as well."

"Why the fuck would you do that?" He told him some cock and bull story about where to bury the bodies. "You had to mention my name when you did that? Mother fuck, Dusty, this is going to get us both locked up for a long time. All I wanted was the money. Money that is as far out of my reach as it's ever been."

"I told you, several times over the last week, to leave with me. To get the fuck out of here before the men you called idiots put two and two together and ended up with us both at the end of a fucking rope. But you just had to have the money." Dusty laughed, and it was bitter and harsh. "Fat fucking lot of good it's going to do us when we're both going to be fried in the chair."

He didn't think this was the time to point out that they didn't use the chair in this state anymore, but lethal injection. Hangings were not used by that many states either. But he left it alone. Dusty was upset enough. As the people used to say about him and Dusty when they'd been kids, don't fucking poke the bear. And poking Dusty right now would be worse than any bear he'd ever seen.

Harley thought about how he could get the fuck out of town. There wasn't any money, no credit cards, and even his stash that he usually had in reserve was gone. The only way he could get out was to hitchhike or to go into hiding. He wasn't stupid enough to think this would die down anytime soon, so he had to think of someplace he could go for a long period of time. Other than prison.

"We need a plan." Dusty said no shit. "Well, while you're ruining my carpet, I'm thinking ahead. We need cash. Enough to set us up someplace that doesn't have extradition. Where?"

"Right off the top of my head I can think of a few. Afghanistan for one. Also Bosnia and Burma." He asked if there was someplace they could go that wouldn't get them killed. "I don't know, dumbass, I don't usually look up places where I can run and hide because it's preferable to prison. I'm more into looking at places to lay my hat, have a good time, to get laid in. Not where I can go so that I don't get my ass shipped home because I've lost all my money."

"You don't need to be so fucking nasty. I'm just trying to figure this out." Dusty said he was sorry, but he was stressed out. "I'm working on getting us taken care of, but we need a plan. One that will get us a little cash to skip town, as well as set us up for a little while. At least until we start making some cash again."

"Kidnapping comes to mind. There is money in that, and you said that the McCulloughs have it." They did, a great deal of it, as a matter of fact. "And there are any number of them to take, too. Why, just the other day I saw that they have babies. We both know that people will do just about anything to get their babies back."

"Yes, I like that idea. That way we can stick it to him

80

twice. Does Larson, my worst nightmare, have any?" Dusty said he didn't know, but could find out. "Never mind. You said that they have babies. Find one of them for me and we'll work from there. And while you're looking into that, I'll see about finding a place to hide it away. This might work. And if it doesn't, we go to prison anyway, right?"

"Yeah, but if it's all the same to you, I'd rather not go to prison. I've done that before, and I have no desire to go back." Harley hadn't been caught so far at anything really seriously bad, thankfully, and didn't want to go either. "I'll do some looking around and see what I can find out about which ones have kids. That way we can do this right."

Harley wondered what sort of lenience he could get if he turned Dusty in for the kidnapping job, and then decided that would be the fall back plan. He didn't want to turn his friend in, but he'd do it in a heartbeat if it came to that. He wasn't going to prison, not if he could help it.

Chapter 6

Virginia loved her new office. And just this morning her things had arrived from her place that she'd shared with her mom. The company that had packed things up had done a great job, and so far nothing had been broken yet. Of course, when you had all the money in the world, she supposed you could hire the best.

She was putting some of her books on the shelf when Lauren and Reese came in. This wasn't good.

"Don't get all tensed up. We've only come to tell you what is going on." She told Lauren that made her tenser. "Yeah, well, I'd be that way too if I had to unpack all this stuff. But then I don't like to write, so it could be that. What the hell kind of money does one make off of putting a few words on paper?"

"Very good money, if you want to know the truth. Enough that I could pay cash for my home, put some money in the bank, and have some fun too." Lauren said that was impressive. "Thank you. I think so as well, since we had nothing before that."

She liked Lauren. She was scary organized and seemed to know more laws and how to break them than she'd bet most criminals did. But she was nice too, when she wanted to be. So far she'd not seen her that way except when she was holding one of her kids. Then she was as mushy as Virginia was about it.

"About why we're here. You should have a seat. I don't have time to go cleaning a mess up if you decide to get all faint on me. There is some trouble that you need to be made aware of." She sat down when Jon and Mac joined them. "They're here to help me soften the blow. And so you know, nothing will happen to Sam."

"Sam? What do you think might happen to him? Come on, tell me." She did. Virginia started to stand, but when she wobbled a bit, she sat again. "And how are you going to prevent this from happening? Or, as you said, him not getting hurt? Because he's not going anywhere unless I'm one hundred percent sure he's not going to be hurt at all."

"I thought you'd tell me no, right off the bat. Sort of took the wind out of my sails." Virginia wasn't sure what to say to her so said nothing. "Anyway, as you know, the office of Harley is bugged, and by doing so, we got a little bit of a heads up on what they're planning to do. Not to kill Sam...at least he's not mentioned it as yet, but I'm not going to rule it out. They're thinking of taking one of our kids, but especially one of Larson's, for ransom. Wells and his partner have no cash, and they think—and this is really stupid on their part—that they can get enough to go to another country and we'll be fine with that."

"No, I'm not fine with any of this." Lauren said she wasn't either. When Virginia looked at the other women, she wondered why they were there. "You others, you're thinking

84

something might go wrong. And you don't want to do this. Or, you think that this plan of hers is great. Either because you're afraid of her or she's going to bully you into her way of thinking. Which is it?"

Mac spoke first. "I think this is the best plan we can do and not have any of the children harmed. However, there are risks involved, as in anything that we might do. But Lauren is good, and that is enough for me to go along with this." She looked at Reese.

"I'm just concerned about what will happen to the baby. Any of them could be hurt by this." Jon said he'd be with whoever was taken. "Yeah, but I don't want you hurt either."

"Tell me the plan." Lauren started talking and told her what was going to happen, what was in place when it did, and where Jon would be during this entire thing. "What if he is hurt?"

"I can't be hurt." She asked him why not. "Because I'm a true immortal, as are you. The entire family is. Not young Sam yet; though he will be when I touch him, but I've not as yet."

She wasn't sure how to take that. Nor exactly what that meant to be a true immortal. But for now, she'd let it go. There were more important things to talk about than whether or not she was going to live or die.

"But you will fix him. And soon, right?" Jon assured her that he would as soon as they were done talking. "All right, so they're going to take Sam, we think, and demand money. Between the taking and me kicking their asses, what is supposed to happen in the meantime?"

"They will only take him long enough to demand money. After that, I'll move in with my men and we'll get the baby back. Then we'll go after Harley and his partner." She asked why he had to demand money first. "Because it makes it a longer sentence when he tries to get money from someone rather than just the taking it. Trust me, there are fine points to all sorts of laws, and this one is the best we can do, for now."

"But you have more that you can get them on." Lauren said that she did. It was making it stick that was the hard part. "So, you don't have what it takes to make them as guilty as they really are. Is that what you're saying?"

"Sort of. We can get them on theft of the money from the company. But without Tom here to testify that the money wasn't given to Wells by Tom or his wife, then he might get away with it. Then there is the actual murder of Tom and his wife. We can't get him on that at all, so far. We have the note from the dead men who we presume killed them, but that doesn't leave us with anything close to what we could have if he had mentioned names." Virginia thought this sounded as full of holes as some of her plots before she read her books again. "Kidnapping will get them both behind bars once they ask for money, and then we can work on them individually to see if one will flip on the other. And I think that this Dusty person is our man."

"Why him? I mean, they both seem to be just as guilty as the other." Lauren told her what she knew. "So you have the smoking gun on other murders, and you're going to use that when all is said and done."

"Yes, and we need to talk to you first about how this is going to work with Sam. Then I need you to talk to Larson. I don't think he's going to be as easy to convince this is going to work as you were." She asked her why not. "He's a numbers man. One that likes to see that things go according to plan. And they will, but only so far. We know that a child will be taken, but not which one. We also know that they're going to demand money. Not how much or how they're going to call us about it. When Larson hears about this, he's going to want to see it all planned out to the letter and think that the bad guy will follow it."

"I think he already knows what is going on, Lauren. He'd been listening in on conversations for the last few days. So, keeping this from him, it's going to be hard, don't you think?" Lauren said she'd known that, but it was the execution that she was not telling him about. "Then I don't understand how you thought I'd be easier to convince."

"Because of what you do for a living. You write books and you have plot twists, things going wrong. You move over them, fix them when you want to enhance the plot, much like I do when I have something going on." She asked if she thought Larson could do that. "Maybe, but this is too important, too close to coming to an end to wait and find out. We need to be ready now, not in a couple of days."

It seemed plausible that this would work. The details, while scary, had the makings of a good story. But she wasn't sure that using little Sam, who had already lost so much, was a good idea. She looked at Jon when he said her name.

"I will be with him at all times. They'll never know it... they'll never suspect that he's got anyone with him." She nodded, then thought of something else. "I can see in your eyes that you're going to turn us down, aren't you?"

"No, I'm not, but I think I have a plan that is going to make everyone, including Larson, happy. You be him. Be Sam." He looked at Lauren and she burst out laughing. "I'm not trying to be funny here, but what better — ?"

"Oh no, you misunderstood. I think that is brilliant. I only wish I had thought of it. Yes, this will work. And since Jon can be anything and do anything, he'll never be harmed, and he can relay any troubles to us as they come along. I love it." Lauren was barking orders to someone on the phone when she looked over at Mac, who smiled.

"You surprised her, again. She's really good-natured about it when someone comes up with a plan better than hers, and she's good about giving credit where credit is due. You did good." Virginia nodded, but wasn't sure what the hell was so funny about it. But if it kept Sam safe, she was all for it.

So, while the plan was reworked, she took Jon to see Sam. He was so beautiful when he slept, and she loved watching him, but there was work to be done too, and she knew that if she stayed in his room all day, she'd not be doing so well in the literary world.

"I need only to be a baby, as I'm sure that neither of them has seen him. But I will be as close to him as I can get." She nodded, and watched him as he picked the baby up, not waking him at all. "He is so tiny, isn't he? I mean, I know that babies are small, but he seems to be so much smaller than the babies that Lauren and Colin have."

"They're older than him by a few months, and I'm not sure that my cousin didn't have some issues when she was pregnant with him too. Plus, with a baby, they change almost daily. I don't know what sort of changes are supposed to happen, but I've been reading about them. I've never been around them before." Jon said that he hadn't either until coming here. "You don't mind doing this, do you? I don't want you hurt either."

He touched his fingers to her cheek, then touched Sam. She felt the power of his touch to her as if she'd been set in some kind of vibrating machine. When he looked at her, she could almost see other creatures in his eyes, and asked him about it.

"They're all there. Few can see them unless I allow them to. The school that I'm going to, they allow me to be whatever I feel like so long as I don't hurt anyone. I would never do that, but I like rules." She said that she did for the most part as well. "I should like for you to have a drop of my blood in your system. That way you can heal much quicker, and you'd be able to protect little Samuel better if the time would ever come."

"Do you think it will?" He said that he did, but not what or when. "Then I'm all right with that. I don't know much about you, nor this family, but I love Larson, and know that he trusts you all. So, in order to be all that I can for all of them, if it only takes a few drops of your blood, then I'm all for that too."

"Thank you. And we love you as well." She nodded and asked him what she needed to do. "Just prick my finger with the needle there. And when you do, lick the wound and all will be well."

"All right." She did as he asked her to do and stared at the blood that was welling up on his finger. "I'm afraid, if you want to know the truth."

"You should be. Forever. But this, it will make you stronger." She nodded and licked his finger. The power of his blood washed over her until she was dizzy with it. "Careful there. You don't want to have to tell your mate that I hurt you, now do you?"

When the baby was put back in his crib, they left his room. There was a monitor in the room and in the one that she had been in. Before leaving, she saw that it was off. Looking up at Jon, just realizing how tall he was, she asked him about it.

"In the event that you turned into a cow or something, I didn't want the others to see you." She asked if she might

89

have. "I don't think so, but you never know about things like this. I'm still figuring things out on my own."

He left her there, at the doorway to the nursery, while she thought of what he'd just said to her. Could she be a cow? Not that she wanted to be that particular animal, but the thought of shifting into something bad-assed really was exciting. Virginia made her way down the stairs thinking about all the things that had happened to her since coming here. Life, she realized, sure did have a lot of plot holes. They were explaining the plan to Larson when she returned to her office. She noticed that no one mentioned the first plan at all. Probably a good thing, she thought.

~~~

Larson loved where his office was in town. However, today he wasn't looking forward to it as he usually did. He was going to his office for the first time in a few weeks, and he was actually sort of nervous about it. Like when he was in school and he'd not go for a couple of days for some reason. Going back would cause him a little unease. But he'd not been in his office since, he thought, about the time he'd been notified that Tom and Donna were dead. He sat at his desk as he thought about what he was doing here.

It wasn't to close up the office, like his first plan had been. Spending time at home, working on the yard and being with Virginia and Sam, made him dread having a job that took him away from them. And really, he could do his job from home just as easily as he could do it from the office.

But as Lauren pointed out, no one was coming to his home to talk business, and inviting others into his home was almost as bad as having them know his personal phone number. It would and could get them into deep shit, as she put it.

He needed to protect them, both Virginia and the baby.

90

Sam was as much a part of his little family as his brothers were, and he had fallen in love with him from the start. And soon, in a few weeks, he was going to adopt him when he married Virginia.

When his phone rang he didn't bother answering it, knowing that the service was still on, but he did open up his computer and started looking through the emails that had piled up. Again, he could have done this from home, but there were no distractions here and he needed to concentrate on work for a bit. There was too much going on right now, and he was overwhelmed.

When one of his family reached out to him, Larson paused in answering an email. He knew who it was, but was almost afraid to hear what Hawkins had to say to him. He was laughing when Larson asked him what he wanted.

Why is everyone so suspicious when I talk to them? Is it my personality, or maybe the fact that I carry a gun?

Larson laughed when he did. *I think it might have to do with the fact that not only do you know how to use that gun better than most do, but that's not all you carry on your person. I think I saw a thin wire, as well as several knives on the table when you were home last.* Hawkins thought it was his charming way of talking to people. *You go on believing that, and I'll sell off the bridge I have at home in the drawer. What's up?*

What do you know, if anything, about money laundering? I mean, in the sense that I don't know how it's done. Larson asked him if he was doing that. *No, but I have an idea that someone is, and I want to make sure that I have all the facts before I go in and be my charming self, and kick the shit out of them.*

Family? He said never. *Okay, to launder money you need bad money, and in that I mean that it's tainted with some bad deed, like drug money. Or even money that they've stolen. It usually has some*

91

sort of tag on it, such as some serial numbers that might be on a list. Or funny money, as in counterfeit. Which does this one fall under?

Counterfeit, and perhaps some drug money too. I'm thinking that he needed to make a deal go down, and printed his own to make sure that he had enough. I think he figures that the people that he got the drugs from won't be able to have him arrested because they'd have to tell what they bought. Larson told him not necessarily. *You mean that you can have someone arrested for dealing in counterfeit money, even though it was used for a drug deal?*

Yes, that's the way some people catch the bad guys. Then when the counterfeiter is arrested, they have a direct line to the dope guys too. Hawkins laughed. *I know, it seems that you're damned if you do and if you're caught. Is there something that I should know about this?*

Nah, just something that I'm working on. I'm not in country, so I figured that if I had to do some fancy footwork on this, I might as well have all the information I can get. By the way, I was wondering if you'd do something for me. Invest my last bonus check into something long term. He said he could do that. Anytime. *I want you to also do some of your magic on some other money that I have. It's not a great deal, but I can invest it into some things around town. Like, I want a place where people can learn self-defense from some of my buddies here.*

I like that idea. I think I might even have the perfect place in mind for you. Larson told him about the old grocery store that had come up on the market. *It has an open plan in it so you can work. There are offices too that you might need, as well as running water and a kitchen, if that is something that you want to work with. Bathrooms can be added, as well as more showers. I love that. I'd like to go in with you on it.*

Deal. Here's something that I'm going to share with you. And don't tell Mom and Dad just yet...I want to surprise them. But I'm leaving the service earlier than I thought. Jarvis will still use me like he does Lauren, but I'll be home for good for the most part by Christmas. That was only in a few weeks or so. *I just don't enjoy this as much as I used to. It's too political.*

Larson thought it was political even before his brother joined up, but as he didn't have a lot to do with it, he held his opinion to himself. As they talked about what he wanted done to the building, Larson made notes. He was as excited as he'd been in a while about any sort of project.

His phone was ringing as he made his way back from the bathroom. He answered it this time, thinking that he could take a couple of calls while he was there. Just as he was ready to take notes on the call, he heard laughter and felt his skin crawl.

"Hello, Larson. It's been a while." The voice was Harley, he knew that from the calls he'd been listening to for Joe. "I want you to know that there are no hard feelings now about the shares that you stole from me."

"I didn't steal anything from you, Harley. I did my job and that's all I did." Harley laughed again. "What is it you think to gain by calling me today? I assure you that what I did for Tom and his wife was done correctly."

"I'm sure you think so. But alas, I have no money, nor did I have anything to do with their murders." Larson told Harley he'd said that before, but later he'd said he'd killed them both. "No, I think you might have misheard me. Or that you made it so that it sounded like that. That sister-in-law of yours, she can be quite good at doing things to suit herself."

That was what Lauren had said he'd do...blame any kind of confession that he'd made on her. Well, he didn't care. Larson knew that Wells had done it, and the sooner the man was behind bars, the happier he'd be about it.

93

"Yes, so I've heard. You never told me why you called me. And I don't believe for a moment that you've called to tell me that you're going to back off and leave me to myself. What did you want?"

"First, I want my money, and for you to keep the police out of this." He asked him why he'd do either of those things. "Because, my dear boy, things could happen to that nice little family of yours. And I'm not worried about you recording this. I know for a fact that you are, and like I said before, that girly of yours, Lauren, she can do whatever she wants to make someone look guilty. Can't she?"

The laughter was still ringing in his head long after Harley hung up. It took every power that he had to simply put the phone back in the cradle it was in without smashing it against the wall. Sitting in his chair, wondering what the fuck was wrong with the world, he barely moved when Jon walked into the room.

"Go away, please. I'm in no mood to be nice, and I'd really hate to have to explain to my mate what happened to me." He asked him what he meant. "Because if you sit there, telling me that things are going to work out, I may have to slug you. Then you're going to do something equally harsh back at me and I'm going to be hurt."

Jon laughed, and that just pissed him off more. Larson wasn't even sure what he was so angry about, but he was and he glared at the phone again. Jon told him to look at him. And when he did, all he could think about was that he was in over his head here.

"I'm not going to hurt you. However, as Mom is forever telling me, violence never solved anything. But Aunt Lauren says that it can sure go a long way in making you feel better. So long as the other guy knows what he's up against. Do you

94

suppose she meant I should tell them what sort of being I am?" He said that no one would believe him until he acted. "Yes, I suppose that's true, but I am here for a reason. I would like for you to teach me how to be an investor."

"I'm thinking of closing up shop for good." Jon asked him why he'd do that. "I don't enjoy it much anymore. I mean, I'll do it for myself and the family, but I don't like being in the position that I'm in now."

"You have a knack, Grandpa says. You can turn a sow's ear into a golden arch. I'm not entirely sure what he means by that, but that's what he is saying. He can be a little hard to understand for me at times." Larson laughed and told him he was hard to understand for all of them. "But I love him dearly. I love you all. However, I would like to understand what you do better."

So, for the next two hours, he told Jon what it was he did and how he made money off of each one of the sales he did for other people. Jon was getting good at predicting things as they looked at the computer, and when they were finished, needing some lunch, they walked over to the little diner in town and saw the for-sale sign had been removed.

"I bought it yesterday with Dad's help. We're going to have it renovated and then give it to Mom for Christmas. She'll have a kitten." Larson said that she more than likely would. "I want her to be happy. She's made me happier than I've ever been. And now with all of you around me, loving me too, I feel like a regular person."

"Yes, well, a regular person that has all these special abilities, one of which will turn you into whatever you want at a moment's notice." They were both laughing as they entered the diner. "So, are you planning to expand this place? I would add about a dozen more booths, as well as an outdoor seating area. I tried to get May to do it, but she said that she had enough on her plate without having to go outside and wait on people. She wasn't a people person, I don't think."

Jon pulled out a sheet of paper that Larson could see was a list of other things that Jon had to do. Jon laughed when he asked him if he really needed to write it down. Jon shook his head and put it away.

"Mom. She likes lists, and to make her feel like I'm paying attention, which I always am, I write things down for her. She can be really intense when she wants to be about things. Like Aunt Virginia. She sure can put a man in his place when she feels the—"

When he stopped talking, he knew that something had happened. Paying for the food by throwing down money, they left as Jon seemed to be listening to someone. As soon as they were outside of the restaurant, he turned to him.

"I have to go be Sam. Now." Larson nodded. "You know your part? You know what you have to do, don't you?"

"Yes. I know. I'll follow the plan." Jon paused in taking off. "What else has happened? Jon, I don't want you hurt."

"Get home and wait. I have to go, but just wait for the man to come to you." He nodded and Jon hugged him. "It'll be just fine, Uncle Larson. Just fine."

Then he was gone. Getting into his car, Larson had to sit there for several moments just to get his heartrate to settle. Someone was going to take his son. Well, not his son, but they thought they were. As soon as he heard from his mom, he knew that things were rolling in the right direction. He just hoped that the bad guys followed the plan too.

Chapter 7

Dusty held the little guy tightly in his arms. He'd never held a child, at least not this small, before and was terrified of dropping him. Putting him on the floorboard so he'd not roll off the seat, he looked at the little guy.

"This just ain't right." The kid, of course, said nothing, but did stare at him with those big blue eyes. "Nothing was ever said about what I was to do with you, and this, this just ain't right. I can't do this."

He started the car and made his way to the McCullough house. Dusty had made a decision that would get him killed, either by the police—who he thought would be kinder in killing him—or Harley. Harley would make him suffer in ways that Dusty didn't want to think about.

"I'm telling you right now, kid, you're lucky as fuck." He glanced over at the kid and wondered why he thought he was understanding every word he said. "They won't believe me when I get there. And if they want, I'll let them kill me off. But I don't want to suffer. I can't stand pain. I'd do just about anything to keep from hurting. Not that I don't deserve it, but

97

I don't want to."

Pulling into the little drive next to the mammoth house, he sat there. There were people walking around the house, all of them with tool belts on and some of them with hard hats. He wanted to be like them, a person that had a good job with benefits. The only benefit he had was that he got a lot of money that he saved up. And now he couldn't even get to that. Things were not as he wanted them to be, that was for sure.

"I don't know why I think you can understand me, and maybe it's just me being scared shitless, but I got me a bunch of money saved up. If you can understand me, I want you to have someone go and get it, and use it for some kind of charity shit. I know that your family does that sort of thing, but you go on ahead and use it for that for me. All right?"

The baby blinked at him, and Dusty was sure as he was sitting there that he'd do it. Reaching down for the little boy, he stared at him and saw intelligence and compassion. Then Dusty realized that the kid wasn't no more than a couple of weeks old at best. That he'd not understood a single word he'd said. Getting out with the baby in his arms, he paused when three large men came out of the house.

"I didn't hurt him, not at all. I brought him to you because of what Harley wanted me to do with him. I can't do that." The first man came toward him, and Dusty put out the child for him. "If you're going to kill me, you should know a couple things first. I have a list of people I've killed, and I'd like to tell you where they are."

"All right." He took the baby from him and handed him to the man behind him. "My name is Larson, and this is my son."

"Yeah, he wanted your baby most of all, but he'd have

taken any of them. I wasn't too squeamish about taking any of them, but I ain't gonna kill them for anyone. That kid didn't do anything wrong other than to be born to you, and I am not going to kill him for Harley, that's the God's honest truth." Dusty let out a long breath as he continued. "There is a chipper at the house that I was to take the baby to. Harley asked me to wait for him to get there, and then he'd kill the kid while we watched. He wanted to throw that little thing in the chipper and watch it.... Well, you can guess what he wanted."

"And you had a change of heart why?" Dusty told him. "You've never killed a child? You want me to believe that?"

"You can or not, but I have never done that. I might have cuffed a couple of them, but I don't kill them. Not a kid... no way, no how. I have me a list of dates and times. Bigger than the one that you might have found in the storage place where I had my guns hidden. You found it, I know. I'll give you that and anything else you want if you can cut me some slack about my prison time. I know I'm going, but I'd like to not be put in general lockdown. I'll not make it." He looked up when a woman came out of the house. She was holding a baby and he nodded to her. "I'm powerfully sorry that I took him. I've been thinking...Well, I guess I should have done some thinking before now, but I want to tell someone everything, right down to where the bodies are. Give them people closure, if you won't mind."

"All right. Will you come into the house? We have everyone ready to take your statement." He wasn't sure how that had happened, but he looked at the baby as he walked by it. It wasn't the same. Dusty didn't know why he thought that, but it wasn't the same baby he had held in his arms. "Are you coming?"

He entered the house and nearly wept with relief. There

99

were others there, FBI, police, as well as a couple of men with DEA written on their chests. Drug Enforcement Administration wasn't one that he'd thought would be around, but he didn't care. They would help him, they all would.

When he was sat down at a large table that still had plastic around the legs, he looked around the big house. It was coming along, nicely too. He could see this big family, gathered around it and having a good time. He envied them in that moment. To have something so normal, so mundane as dinner together, was something that he'd never experienced with a family. He had no one.

"Do you think I could have something to drink? Not booze, though that would help, but just some tea or something? I have a lot to tell you, and I'm thirsty from being so nervous." Not only did they bring him a large glass of iced tea, but he had a plate of scones too. Dusty touched the pretty plate and started to cry. It was just too much, the kindness of these people. "I'm not a nice person. I didn't have to be like this, but it was easier to be a bully than it was to be nice. And it got me things. I'm a failure at life." He cried harder than he had in his entire life.

"Mr. Crane, would you like a moment?" He shook his head, then nodded at the woman. "My name is Lauren McCullough. Are you armed?"

"Yes. I can get them if you'd just not shoot me yet." She said she wouldn't if he wasn't stupid. "I've been that my whole life, ma'am. I don't think I know how to be anything else, but I'll get it off my chest now and you can do with it what you want."

After being disarmed, he was put into cuffs. It was something that he expected, but it made him feel like a criminal and so out of place in this grand house. He looked around the place again and then at Lauren.

"Harley Wells and I grew up in an orphanage. Neither of us were adoptable. We were what you might call the violent type. My parents were druggies, and both of them died when I was just a little thing. Harley was left there when he was just a baby…his momma never turned herself in or anything, and probably knew that he was going to be a handful." Lauren nodded, but didn't say anything. "I'm not going to tell you a lie about anything we did together. You have to know that we weren't treated well at the orphanage, and when we got out, nearly the same time, we didn't have any skills to teach us to be any different than we had there, mean and stealing. Times were different then, so we had a difficult time of it. Anyway, I'll start with the Simmonses."

"All right, tell me how you were involved in their deaths." He said that he wasn't. "Mr. Crane, you said you'd not lie to me."

"I didn't even know what he was going to do until it was a done deal. I thought he was just going to rough them up a little, then take them someplace to be found later. The boat, and their deaths, it was all him. I did help him with the two men that were killed afterwards, but not the couple." She started writing things down. "We had money. Or I do. Harley never could save a nickel when he could use it to try and make himself a quarter. I didn't spend anything that I made, and let me tell you, that was harder than you think. Anyway, when I heard that he'd killed them, I went to him to find out why. That's when I learned about the shares. To be honest, I figured he was going to take them without me knowing and disappear, but he was fooled with, and that pissed him off."

"Do you know where the money is?" He said that he didn't. And didn't know what the amount was until Harley

101

told him. "Did you at any time have any contact with the Simmonses when they were alive?"

"No. I wouldn't know them if they were here. I told you, I didn't know a thing about their being killed until afterwards. Harley, he has a temper, and he would say he was going to do things but he never got around to it." She asked him if he had done anything for him. "Yes, a lot of times. I was his hitman, I guess you could say."

He told them everything he could think of about the Simmonses' deaths. Even how Harley had asked him to find the kids so he could see if they had it. But Dusty had never told him that he'd found the kids and left them alone. He could see how they were grieving, and he just couldn't bring himself to hurt them anymore.

As they talked about the events of today, he nodded. "I asked him to take me out to the place I was to meet him. I don't know how to read well, so directions don't mean all that much to me. But once we got there, I could see that there was a brand-new chipper there. You know, one of those things that you put trees in and it comes out the other side like mulch. I asked him about it."

"What did he say?" Dusty sat there, fingering the sweat on the glass he had. He thought about what Harley had said, and how he'd said it. "Mr. Crane?"

"He told me that he'd bought it for this occasion. I wasn't sure what he meant. Like was he finally going to clear cut the trees? I knew that he had the property, but I'd never been there before. Harley told me over and over that he had that place, and that it was overgrown with trees and stuff. Bushes." He looked at the woman. "Let me do this in my own way, please? I can't...it's hard to talk about what he said, I mean."

"All right. Take your time." He nodded. "Would you

like more to drink? I have some whiskey you can have if you want."

"Yes, I'd like that." She got up, but he wasn't thinking that he'd be able to follow her. There were six armed men in the room with him, and each of them looked ready to go to war. When she returned, she gave him a shot glass and a bottle of whiskey. The good stuff too. He poured himself a shot of it and drank it down before speaking again.

"Harley took me out to the farm, as he called it. I don't know why. There didn't seem to be any cows or nothing there. Just scrub and trees, lots of trees. The house was in poor repair, but no different than what we grew up in, I guess. But there was this chipper by the barn. Still all wrapped up and shiny red." He poured himself more whiskey and then drank it down. His hands were shaking worse than they'd been when he'd been told about the kid and what was going to happen to it. "He said that I was to bring the kid to him there, and to wait for him. He had to establish himself an alibi or something. Anyway, he ran his hand over the thing and said, just like he was telling me what he'd had for breakfast, that he was excited as fuck to watch the splatter come out the other end. I wasn't sure that was what he was saying, so I asked him, right out. 'You killing that kid in this?' Harley looked crazy then, and nodded. Said it was payback to that McCullough that took his money."

Dusty drank two more shots before he thought he could go on. And when he did, he told them how he'd picked up the baby and brought it straight here. He said he had more to tell, but right now, he needed to just sit and think for a moment.

"Does he know that you're here?" He shook his head and pushed the glass away. "We want you to take him the child, Mr. Crane."

"Are you fucking insane? I just told you what he was going to do with it. You want him to kill this kid anyway?" She said no, but he'd be all right. "How am I gonna be all right? I will hand him over this kid and watch him kill it. I might be a lot of things, lady, but I'm not a murderer of little babies."

She turned and looked at the younger man when he entered the room. "This is Jon. He's special. I want you to watch him, and then I'll explain to you what we want you to do. All right?"

He nodded and watched the kid. When he shifted into a wolf, he sat there with his hands gripping the table. And as the kid shifted into several other animals, all Dusty could think about was that he was special all right. Scary special. Then when he took a step toward him and knelt down, Dusty looked into his face.

"I'll do just what you wanted." Then he was the baby, just lying there on the floor looking up at him with the same face, the same intelligent eyes, and everything. He looked at the woman again when she said his name. Dusty had a feeling it hadn't been the first time she'd said it either.

"You'll take Jon as the child. He will make sure that you and he are both safe, but we need to catch Harley at this. Otherwise it'll be you that goes down, not him." He asked about the other deaths, the ones that he'd committed too. "You let me worry about those when this is done. Right now, we have to get you on the road to where you're to meet him."

Jon, now a kid again, followed him out to the car. He was shaking so bad now that Dusty wasn't sure he could drive them there in one piece. But when Jon touched him, just put his hand on his shoulder, he calmed a great deal. But it was his smile that told him things were going to be all right.

"You'll be fine, Dusty. Just trust me." He nodded and said that he'd really had no choice. "Yes, you did, and you made a good one. Just follow the instructions like Aunt Lauren told you, and you'll be fine. I promise."

Nodding, he got into this car. It was as good as he was going to get, a promise from a kid no more than fifteen or so years old. But to look at him, deep into his eyes, Dusty thought he was older, and even older than himself. Whatever happened, he felt better about the fact that he'd went this route rather than with Harley. But Harley was surely going to be pissed off when he figured it out.

~~~

Harley was ready to call Dusty again when he saw the dirt flying up behind a car. He was so excited that he'd been nursing a hard-on for the last two hours. All he needed to do was call Larson and demand the money. After that, he'd be gone in the wind and nobody would ever find him.

The kid was asleep, and that suited him just fine. Dusty said that he'd gotten lost, but it mattered little to him. As soon as he disposed of the kid, he was going to run his friend through the same chipper. They'd be picking up pieces of these two for years and never find them all. Dusty asked him what he'd done. Harley looked at the blood stain that had been a stranger no more than an hour ago.

"I had to see if it worked, didn't I? I didn't want to come all the way out here and find out that the stories I'd read weren't true. So I had a test run." He giggled when he saw Dusty looking at the field of blood. "I was surprised at how fast it went. I mean, with this kid, we'll have to be watching close or we'll miss it."

"Harley, who was that?" He said he didn't know him, but that he'd been wandering around the yard when he'd gotten here. "So, you just asked him to get into the thing and he did it without any troubles?"

"No, moron, I killed him first. Christ, what is wrong with you? You act like you haven't ever seen a dead body before." Dusty said nothing, but continued to stare at the bloody grass. "I tell you, Dusty, this is the best plan that I've ever come up with. I'll get the money and get to take out my revenge too."

He looked at the kid and decided that it was the ugliest baby he'd ever seen. He pointed out some of its flaws to Dusty, who just shrugged. He asked him again what was wrong with him.

"Nothing. Just make the fucking call so we can get out of here. I don't like it out here. We're sort of exposed, don't you think?" He supposed that they were a little, and pulled out his cell. Taking several pictures of the baby, he asked Dusty if he was doing it right. "You should take one of you and him, so he knows that you got him."

"Good idea." He handed his phone to Dusty. "Make sure that you take one where you can see his face. I don't want him to be thinking that it's just any old baby I got. Oh, and you have to show me how to send it. I never can get that part to work."

When the picture was sent with his demands, he giggled again. He'd been doing that most of the day today, just giggling like a kid with a new toy. The baby gurgled a little and he looked down at it. There was something about the kid that made him uncomfortable. But when his phone rang, he answered it with a smile.

"Hello, Larson. You got my message, I guess." Dusty took the baby from him and sat on the ground with it. He sure was acting weird. Harley missed what Larson said and asked him to repeat it.

"You kidnapped the wrong baby." He thought he meant that he had the wrong kid and nearly asked Dusty about it when Larson continued. "You have fucked with the wrong people, Harley. And when I get there, you'll pay."

"You'll be the one paying, moron. Just bring me that forty million in cash and I'll give you the kid. But you'd better hurry, I might drop him or something, and that'd be a shame, don't you think?" Larson said nothing, but he wasn't worried. "Just gather up your money and come here to give it to me. And once you're gone, I'll tell you were the kid is."

He giggled again. This time he had to cover his mouth because it didn't seem to want to stop. Harley was a little worried about that, like he was going crazy or something, but when Larson said he was coming, he put his phone away and looked at Dusty.

"It's been a real pleasure working with you, buddy." He nodded, but didn't look up when he pulled out his gun and pointed it at him. "Dusty, I can't have you taking some of my profits. I'm really sorry about this."

"You do what you gotta do." That didn't sound right, and he asked for the third time if he was all right. "I am, better than I think I've ever been. You're the monster in all this, Harley. To think that you was going to put that little baby in that thing over there, it makes me glad that I'm not going to be with you."

"What do you mean? You can't have figured out what I was going to do." Dusty said it didn't matter. "Yes, it does. You think you know me so well? Well, you don't. I'm not saying I'm not going to kill you, but you have to know that it's for the best."

"The best for who, Harley? The only person making out with this is you. And so you know, I just don't care what you do with me after today. You were gonna kill this kid and that, in my book, makes you a monster. A monster is what you are." He told him to take it back. "I don't think so. Shoot me, I couldn't care less."

He shot at him three times, each of them coming closer and closer to his feet, but Dusty never flinched, didn't move out of the way of the bullets, nor did he beg him to stop. It was as if he really didn't care what happened to him. It was then that he noticed that the blanket and the kid were missing. He looked around and didn't see it, then looked at Dusty again.

"What did you do with that kid?" Dusty only sat there. "Did you hear me? What did you do with that kid, Dusty? If you tell me right now, I'll hurry and shoot you in the head. Where is it at?"

"He's standing behind you." Dusty looked at him then smiled. It was creepy and sad looking. "He's not no kid either, Harley. I think he's going to make you wish that you'd never been born."

Turning slowly, he tried to think what Dusty had meant by that. The kid couldn't stand, it could barely hold its head up, but when he turned around, he looked at the thing behind him, and it took his befuddled mind a few seconds to figure out what he was seeing.

"It's a dragon. A fucking dragon." He stood there for several seconds more, and decided that it wasn't real. Reaching out his fingers to touch whatever this was, he felt the heat of it roll across his hand. "Well, ain't you about the best thing in the world? I bet I could make a few bucks off you too. Wanna be my partner?"

The monster moved his head upward, towering over him about six more feet than his already tall stance. When he roared out, flames spraying from his mouth, Harley could

108

barely contain his excitement. He had a dragon. A real live dragon. And when the dragon moved his head down to his level, the heat of his roar touched him.

It was warming, wonderfully hot, to be touched by a dragon. But when he started to feel too much heat, he put out his hand again to stop him. To tell him that it was enough, to turn off the fire.

The flames licked at his body harshly. His clothing was on fire now, and no amount of stomping his feet would stop it. As he used his hands to stop the fire, he noticed that they were on fire as well, that flames came from his fingers like they had from the dragon's mouth. Turning to look at Dusty, to tell him what he was feeling, he saw the look of horror on his face and decided that he was a prude. Harley had a dragon.

The pain started then, even after the dragon disappeared, the boy standing before him taking his place. Dropping to his knees, he was sick with the pain now. There were blisters on his hands, and his clothing was still burning. Everywhere he touched himself parts of his pants and shirt came off. It was then that he noticed that his fingers were missing, his hand was falling off, and he was unable to speak or see very well.

Lying down on the ground, he wondered what was going on. All he wanted to do was get his money and then watch as the kid was killed. It would have been like an art show for him. As his body became more and more painful, he knew that he was dying. Harley was saddened by that…he didn't get to buy his own island to live on.

Chapter 8

Larson wasn't sure what he was supposed to do now. He sat, rocking Sam in his arms, as the rest of his household moved around him. It wasn't until his mom came and sat in front of him that he thought about speaking, though unsure what he wanted to say, but he did need to talk.

"Jon is learning the business, but I'm not sure that I'm going to keep doing it. It's dangerous. I'd like to have Thanksgiving here next year, if you don't mind. I don't think I'll be ready for it this yearnow, but if it is, I'd very much like to host it this year. The house is still under construction but it's coming along nicely, don't you think?" She said it was and mentioned that the baby might need his diaper changed and to be fed. "Not yet. I can't let him go just yet. When he cries, then someone can take him for a few minutes, but I need him here."

"All right, son. You just rock him then." He did, back and forth in the big rocker that his mom had brought him a couple of days ago. "Would you like something to eat? Or to drink?"

"No, I'm not ready for that. I have to get the office done

for myself. I don't think I'm going to do the job anymore. It's lost its appeal for me. I might do something else, like work for Reese. Did you know that they bought her the building?" Mom said that she did know that. "I don't think she'll care if I come in and bus tables or something, do you?"

"No, she'd probably like the extra help. Larson, we have to talk about what is going on with you." He nodded and rocked harder, waking Sam up. "Careful, son. You don't want him to cry, do you?"

"No, I don't want him hurt." He rocked slower, this time looking at his little face. "He was going to put him in the shredder. I know that's what Dusty said, but he really was going to put a little child in that thing to see him die. Mom, I can't stand that."

"But he didn't, because Jon made sure that he wasn't harmed." He nodded, but didn't look at her. She had been crying too, and he wasn't ready for.... He really just wasn't ready. For what, he didn't know, but whatever it was, he didn't want anything to do with it. "Larson, let me take Sam to be fed and changed. All right?"

"Will you bring him back to me?" She said that she would. "Mom, don't let him go. You have to make sure that you bring him back to me. I need him."

He might have closed his eyes for a moment or two. They were burning now, and he wasn't sure if he was seeing things well. When he felt the sting of a slap, he put his hand over his cheek at the pain of it and looked at Virginia. Larson started to ask her what she thought she was doing when she spoke.

"You're scaring everyone. Talk to me." He said that she'd hit him. "Yes, I did, and will again if you don't try and snap out of this. Your dad is terrified that you're going off the deep end. I'm afraid that you're going to leave me here and wander off. Talk to me, Larson. I love you."

"He was going to kill him." She said that he didn't though. "What sort of sick person is all right with just wanting to kill a little baby? One that can't even hold his own bottle. Not that killing an older child is any different, but why, Virginia? Why would that be all right with him?"

"Jon said that he thought that at some point Harley went off the reservation, that his mind had snapped. We don't know, and will never know when that occurred, but he wasn't right in the head. Not at the end, anyway." Larson nodded. He wasn't agreeing or disagreeing with her, just acknowledging that she was talking. "Larson, you're going to have to come to terms with this. You've been sitting here for two days. And when you're not rocking Sam, you're holding a pillow like it's him. Come back to me."

"Two days?" She nodded and wiped at her tears. "I just don't want him hurt. I have to be able to protect him, and I didn't."

"Larson, you did protect him. Don't you see? You didn't allow him to leave the house, and you let Jon take care of the monster that would have hurt him. But he's not hurt. Neither of them are." He looked for Sam and asked where he was. "Larson James McCullough, I'm going to leave your ass here if you don't straighten yourself up."

"Where is Sam? Mom said she'd bring him back to me." He rocked, holding onto the little pillow, his own mind shutting off. "When he's diapered and ready, I'd like to hold him."

Larson noticed that the room was dark. At some point, he supposed that it had gotten dark outside. Rocking again, yelling for his mom to bring Sam back to him, he realized then that he was all alone in the house. There wasn't a single sound anywhere around him. Getting up, sore and achy after sitting there, he hobbled to the kitchen to find his mom.

There wasn't anyone around in there either, but there was a note on the counter from Virginia. He decided to get him a drink, having only just realizing that he was dry to the bone. After refilling his glass twice, he took the envelope to the dining room and sat down at the table. The lights were better in there, and he opened it to read where she'd gone.

"I'm leaving you. I know that's not the best course of action, considering that you're going to turn rogue, but as I can see it now, you've hit that point already." He wasn't sure that was right, but he really didn't know how long he'd been there alone. "I've left you on Saturday afternoon. I don't know what day it is today, but you'd been sitting in the chair, rocking a pillow, for three days before that. I need stability in my life, and you aren't giving it to me right now. I know you hurt, but why, I can't figure out. We have Samuel.

"Have a good life, Larson. I love you with all my heart." Then she signed it Virginia. He got up to find out the date, and was dismayed to find that his phone, at some point, had died. He put it on the charger and reached for Colin.

You all right now? You fucking shit, you scared the hell out of all of us. He asked him the date. *The date? It's the tenth. Why?*

No, the day of the week. Virginia said in a note that she left me on a Saturday. What day is it now? Colin didn't answer him, and that scared him a little bit more. *Colin, she's left me.*

I would have too. The way you were acting made me want to knock the shit out of you to bring you around. He said he was sorry. *Not as sorry as you'll be if you don't fix this with your mate. It's Friday.*

Friday? It had been a week and he'd just been sitting there? He wondered a few things, like how had he not wet himself, but his brother answered that one by telling him that was all he'd done. Got up to go to the bathroom, only to return to the rocker and go back and forth. Holding a fucking pillow.

Where is she? Where is Virginia? He didn't answer him. *Please, Colin. I need to find her. And I need to make this up to her. I don't know what happened to me.*

No one does, Larson. You zoned out and terrified us all. He said he was sorry again, but he was awake now. *She's here. And you should know that she's making arrangements to go back to her old place. So if I were you, I'd clean up, because I'm betting you stink, and come see her. And not empty handed, either.*

Yes, flowers and chocolate. Anything as long as I'm not empty-handed.

He made his way to the bathroom in their bedroom and noticed in a distracted sort of way that the room was finished. That the furniture looked really good. Turning on the water, he noticed that he'd grown a beard, as well as his face looked gaunt. "I suppose not eating for over a week will do that to you."

It took him nearly an hour to shower twice and find himself something to wear. He had clothing, but it wasn't what he wanted to wear. When you went to ask the person you loved more than anyone to come back to you, you should be wearing more than just a pair of jeans and a T-shirt. And a suit just seemed to be too much. So he went for casual funk. He had to wear a belt on his jeans too because he'd lost that much weight.

The florist couldn't have been more helpful to him. He'd only had to tell her that he'd fucked up…not in those words, but close enough that she ran around the store picking out things he needed. Larson was sure that it was too much, just a tad, but they were both having so much fun that he didn't care what the cost was. And then he headed over to the bakery to get something sweet.

Larson had to drive over to Colin's. He'd never been so nervous and shaky in his whole life. Nervous because he was afraid she'd tell him to go fuck himself, which was no less than he deserved. And shaky because he was starving to death. He sure hoped he was going to hit the dinner time hour, because he could easily eat a horse.

Driving carefully, he thought about all the things he wanted to say to her. He loved her would be the first thing, then he'd ask her—no, beg her—to forgive him and take him back. Larson didn't know what he'd done, other than to zone out, but he knew that he'd hurt her. And badly. As soon as he pulled into the drive, he had to sit here for several minutes to make his body stop humming with the shakes.

You going to sit out there all day, or get your ass in here and be a man about the shit you pulled on her? He grinned at the sound of Lauren's voice. *You heard me, so answer me, dumbass. What's it going to be?*

I'm not well. She told him he was going to be a lot less well when he got inside. *No, you don't understand. There's something wrong with me. I mean, I don't think I've eaten for several days, and I can hardly hold on to the steering wheel, I'm so weak.*

Stay where you are.

He could almost feel the concern in her voice, and it touched something deep inside of him. Laying his head back on the headrest, Larson closed his eyes. He really didn't feel well, and when his door opened to his left, he didn't bother looking.

"Here, drink this." Mac turned his face toward her as the other door opened. "Virginia is going to sit with you while you drink this down. It's orange juice, and there are some

116

crackers and cheese. Don't eat it too fast or you'll be sick."

"All right." He looked over at Virginia. "Hello, my dear heart."

She glared at him, then laid her head on his shoulder. "You are an asshole. I had all these things that I wanted to say to you, blast you with, and now I can't because you don't feel well." He told her that he was sure it would pass. "No, I'm pretty mad at you. What happened to you?"

"I don't know. I really don't. All I could think about was seeing him dead. Picking up his little lifeless body and it being cold in death. I've never had anything affect me like that before." Virginia told him that it had felt like that to her when he'd left her there. "I can't tell you how sorry I am that I did that to you. I should have been happy that he was all right. That the family came together and helped us. But I couldn't shake the feeling that he was dead."

He drank down the juice and was handed another one, then Mac left them. He was still not feeling well, but he wasn't as shaky as he had been. As they sat there, he thought of some of the things that had entered his head while he'd been zoned out. It was all he could think to call it, he was zoned out.

"Wells is dead, correct?" Virginia told him that he was. "And his friend, Dusty, where is he now? I have the feeling that he's not."

"No, he's currently working with the police and a lot of other agencies in cleaning up a lot of cold cases. Then he's going to go away for a very long time. I guess life without parole. But for some reason, and Lauren agrees with me, he won't be in there long. He'll try and end his life. This whole thing, it's affected him more than anyone else." She looked at him. "Other than you, I guess. I've missed you."

"And I you. I don't know how to tell you just how sorry

117

I am." He turned when she did and saw the flowers and chocolate. "Well, I was going to try and butter you up with this stuff to have you let me back into your life."

"Chocolate works." She pulled the box to her lap and laughed. "Where the hell did you find a ten-pound box of chocolate? I'm sure that it's not something people just have around."

"I got it at the bakery. They were going to melt it down for some other things, but when I explained what a fuck up I was, they helped me out by making the little blocks of it prettier. Open it and look." She did and laughed harder. "I don't know that I'd approve of it, but under the circumstances, I think it's perfect."

The blocks spelled out asking her for forgiveness. Actually, what it said was, "I'm an idiot. Please forgive me." As she sampled some of the pieces, he ate the cheese and crackers. After the third bottle of juice, he was beginning to feel like he could walk without falling over.

Virginia helped him into the house and into his brother's living room. They were all there, even Jon, and no one of them looked very happy with him. He decided that the truth, in this case, was better than anything he could tell them.

"I was in grief. I don't know why, but it struck me as strange or something, and I thought Sam had been killed. It's all that kept going through my head, that he was gone and his body was lifeless." Jon said that he'd never even been harmed. "I don't think I could get that into my head. It was.... When Wells was talking, all he could talk about was killing him. Running him through that machine and seeing him coming out the other end. Like he had the other man. And I just couldn't get over that. He had died, and that was all I could see."

~~~

Virginia was ready to forgive him when he'd pulled into the driveway. She was still hurt, but hearing him explain things, how he'd felt, to his family, she knew that he was hurt by himself more than he had hurt her. He had completely lost those days when he'd been in his grief, and it cut deep into her heart as well.

The nanny, who was helping her with little Sam as well as the other children in the house, handed Sam to her. She took him right to Larson and put him in his arms. Taking his blanket off and unzipping his jammies, she showed him that he was unharmed.

"See? There isn't a thing wrong with him." He nodded, touching his fingers lightly to his down covered chest and face. "He's been sort of a pain in the butt since we've come here. For some reason, he hates to be rocked anymore."

He laughed. It was so surprising to her that she laughed as well. Larson took his clothing off, leaving him still in his diaper. She wasn't worried about him catching a chill, the room was very warm with all the others in it with them.

"When I saw him, before, it was as if he were lifeless." She said she was sorry for that. "Yes, I don't know why. I know that I keep saying that, but I really don't. I might need a doctor or something."

Jon came to stand with them and gently put his open hand on Larson's head. She wasn't sure what he was going to do, help or hurt him, but she pulled the baby into her embrace while he did it. Just as gently as he touched him, he pulled away and Larson looked up at his nephew.

"You aren't going to need any help with a doctor. You have it all right here." Larson nodded at Jon, as if he believed him. "You need to take a break, Uncle Larson. With the death

119

of your friends and stressing about the baby and your new mate's safety, you were overwhelmed by it all, and it took its toll on you."

"Yes, I need to do something that has nothing at all to do with death and money and anything related to Wells." Jon said that's what he wanted him to do. "I will. First thing I want to do is get married. And I think the sooner the better."

He leaned down to Virginia and kissed her hungrily, then lifted his head enough that her nose was touching his. She heard his belly growling then, and his face lit up with the sound. Giggling, she stood up with Sam and put out her hand to Larson.

"How about you eat first? Then we'll see how you go from there." Dinner was all ready to go, and she headed there with him. "I love you, Larson. I'm glad you're going to be spending time with us. I've missed you."

Dinner was a large noisy affair. They were all there except for Hawkins, who was coming home in a couple of days to visit. Then, according to Larson, he was home for good after that. They'd be a family again, and she knew that Rich and Bea would be happy to have all their *boys* home too.

After dinner was finished and the mess of it cleaned up, they went home. She had left the house with nothing but the things on her back and Sam's diaper bag, so it was nice to get back and into her own things. Having a bed that she loved, and some of the things that she'd brought to the house were amazing to have again. And her mom said that she'd take care of Sam through the night to give them both a much-needed full night's sleep.

"We're not going to get much rest, I'm afraid." She asked him why not, and he wiggled his brows at her. "I haven't been with my mate for a very long time. And neither has my cat.

We've missed you."

"You did, huh? Well, I've missed you both as well." She walked to the bed, opening her robe as she did so. "I just couldn't find a thing to wear that didn't make me want less on. So, I ended up naked for you. Is that all right?"

"More than all right. If you come here, my cat will show you how we feel about that." She didn't even get the chance to move before he was his cat. And then, when he jumped onto the bed with her, she put her fingers into his fur, holding him to her as he purred. It was going to be a long night at this rate, and she couldn't wait to—

"What is it? Sam? Is he all right?" His cat was standing over her, his body stiff, his fur standing straight up as he watched her. "You're freaking me out a little here."

You're in heat. She asked him what that meant. Somewhere in the back of her mind she knew, but when he spoke again, she warmed. Then he was Larson again, his body stiff over hers as he explained. "You're in heat, and if we have sex, we're going to create a child. As much as I'd like to just take you, it's ultimately your decision to have a child."

"Because it's my body." He nodded and she looked into his eyes. They were dark with passion, and something more. She was sure it was need, but she could also see his love for her. "I want to have your child, Larson, more than anything in this world."

He entered her slowly. It wasn't sex, not this time, but making love. And he did it so well. Larson touched her face as he kissed her. Held her in his arms as he made love with her. She felt valued. Loved and happy. And when she felt her climax taking her, it wasn't a hard punch to her body, but a rising up and touching the stars, then brought back to earth on a cloud of feathers.

121

When she cried out with her second release, he held her as he filled her. Giving her something that she would love and cherish for the rest of her life.

"I so love you, Virginia." He held her for the rest of the night, making love to her when he woke, making her feel as if she were the best thing in the world to him. And she felt the same way about him, and would forever.

The next morning she woke to an empty bed. His side was cold, so she knew that he'd been up for some time. When she got up to take her shower, she found a note on the counter top, as well as a pair of worn work gloves.

We need to sort out the stuff in the barn...that's where I am now. If you want to join me, make sure you wear something that you don't mind getting ruined. There were two big hearts, then more to the note. *I am so excited about seeing you heavy with our child. And just in the event that it didn't work, I think we should make sure whenever we can that you are pregnant.*

More hearts and his name. She was still laughing when she got out of the stall and started to dress. Going to the kitchen, she found that her mom was there with the new cook and holding Sam. She held the little boy while her own breakfast was made.

"Do you really want me staying here?" Virginia asked her if she wanted to stay with them. "I do, but the two of you, you have to start your life now, and I don't want to be in the way."

"My goodness, Mom. How can you ever think that? You are my rock when I'm writing, and Larson would never understand me while I'm in my zone." She nodded. "Mom, do you want to live here with us? I can't think of life without you here with me. I don't think I could write without knowing that you were taking care of me."

"You're just saying that because it's true." They both

laughed. "I would love more than anything to live here with you two, and Sam. I've so enjoyed this house and watching it come together. And the room that has been set up for me is simply beautiful. I have my own entrance and shower. Larson even set it up so that I have a kitchen if I want something, as well as a living room. It's like I'm living with you, but not."

"Larson said that he was worried you'd not like living in the lower levels. But you're right, it's really nice, and the fact that it's all yours, I love that too. You can go away and be on your own whenever I get to be too much for you." Mom took Sam when Virginia was given a plate of food. "Mom, please don't leave us. I don't even want to think about you even just being down the street. I love having you around, and Larson thinks the world of you."

"I know that, honey, but as I said, you'll be getting married soon, and you might not feel that way after a few months." She told her never, she was her best friend. "And I love you as well. But let us change the subject. I understand that the two of you are working in the barn today. The pack women are going to be sitting Sam today. He'll enjoy that. They hold him a great deal."

"Yes, they love him too. And he's part of their pack, I guess. Larson said that the more of them that hold him, they'll have his scent and they can find him anywhere." She shivered when she thought of the necessity of that. "You can join us if you want."

"No thanks. I have to go and find me a nice bed and furniture for my living room. Larson said that there is an account at the local mall's furniture shop that I'm to use. What a wonderful man you have in your life." Virginia told her that he was in both their lives. "Yes, I suppose he is. My son-in-law. What a wonderful thing to just realize. Anyway, I'm off

123

to go shopping, and Bea is going with me. We're going to do a little shopping for the holidays. I've never been so excited before."

When her mom left to head to the mall, Virginia put Sam down for his nap. He was just dozing off when three women from the local pack showed up to take care of her little man. Having so much family, extended and otherwise, was something she'd have to get used to. They were all so willing to put out a hand to help you, no matter what was going on.

Chapter 9

Larson pulled the next box of books down and looked at the titles. The lady that had collected these had an eclectic taste in reading. They went from scientific methods of thinking to romance. There was even a sprinkle of children's books among them. He pulled the first book out that he touched and read the title to Virginia.

"What do you suppose she was thinking about when she was reading how to wire a refrigerator for the household?" She said that she didn't know, but apparently, she had dabbled in pottery as well. "Yes, there's a kiln, a gas one, in the barn that Mom wants to play around with. I swear she gets into more things than the kids, but she has fun too."

"Your mom is a hoot, and I love the fact that she includes my mom in a lot of her activities. I've never seen mine so outgoing before. Do you think I stifled her a little?" Larson wondered where she might have come up with that, but before he could answer her, she said his name softly. "Look at this. It's a first edition from William Poe. And it's signed."

They looked the book over and Larson thought it was in

perfect condition. None of the pages were even molded or bent. As they set that one aside, they found four more books, all of them signed by different authors and made out to Miss Jane.

"What was the name of the person that owned this house? Not the sister, who should be shot for leaving all this out here unattended, but the original owner." Larson told Virginia that he might have known at one point, but he didn't anymore. "We should look for their family. I mean, this is some very valuable stuff, maybe they'd want it."

"There wouldn't be anyone left. I mean, not of either sister. They weren't all that kind or nice, and they neither one had ever married, from what I understood from the banker. That's why the house was empty for so long. There wasn't anyone around to tell the bank what to do with it." Virginia said that was sad. "It really is, but I will have someone look for some information on them. The library has some back issues of the town's paper. Perhaps there is something in those."

Virginia seemed excited to have something to look into. She enjoyed research and making sure that her books were done well in that respect. As he pulled the next box off the shelf, avoiding the books for now, he opened the large crate up and looked at the dishes that were inside.

"Virginia, look at these." Larson pulled a plate off the top of the crate and unwrapped it. "Wow, these are beautiful. Look at the detail on this."

The plate that he held had a scene on it of the house they were living in. Not only was the house in color, but the flowers and trees around it were in full bloom too. The next few plates made him realize that someone had painted them by hand… each plate was slightly different. Virginia took the next item and found that it was a tea cup and saucer.

"These are the famous roses, I'm betting." Each one of the little cups was decorated in full color with the roses that he'd been told were prized roses in his back yard. Picking the crate up, they went to the house and put it on the long table in the library that they'd been using to put some of the books on the shelves. As they unearthed all the plates in the crate, he went to get the next three crates to finish the set.

Fourteen place settings were unwrapped, each with a dinner plate, dessert plate, cup, and saucer, as well as a mug and soup bowl. Also, there was a starter set, which he never understood the name of, as well as a large tureen, ladle, and wine glasses that were etched with the same rose design as the cups. And a tea pot that was so delicate he was afraid of breaking it by holding it too tightly.

As they set them out, stacking them in neat piles, all he could think of was the cost it might have been, even back all those years ago. Now it would be a fortune to have such a beautiful handmade set...he couldn't imagine how someone would have justified something like this. Flipping the plate over, he saw the mark and that they were made in his home town.

"Do you think anyone that worked there would remember these plates?" He pulled his computer into the room they were in and started doing a search. "It went out of business in the early fifties after being in business for over one hundred years. There's a website for their company. Market Holland. I'm going to email them."

He'd never imagined that it would be this much fun unearthing boxes of stuff. They had already found so much that they had decided to keep in the house that they had nearly filled an entire room with the boxes. The books would be cleaned and put on the shelves in this room, along with some of the smaller pieces of handmade pottery that they'd found.

By lunchtime they had barely made a dent in the things that were only in the one section of the barn. Dad and the crew working on the house were finishing up the dining room today, and Larson wondered if there was any kind of cabinet that they could display the dining ware in. Eating his sandwich, he looked up when his dad joined him in the kitchen and sat down with a worrisome look on his face.

"What is it, Dad? Please tell me that you're not finding something wrong." He shook his head. "Then what has you looking like you've lost your friend?"

"I was just out in that shed, and I tell you, son, that sucker is huge for just being called a shed. Anyhoo, I found this here stash of furniture clear in the back. I was just wondering how we missed that. But my thinking is, we should hold off on finishing up in there until you two have a look see. I think you might want to make a few changes." He asked why. "Well, it looks like someone just up and tore out some of the pieces that go in there and stuffed them in that shed."

They spent the next three hours going through the building. Dad found some pieces that he could use in the house, mostly built-ins, and they found many boxes of love letters, as well as several from the government on the death of a son. But the best part was, they had a few names to work with. And Miss Jane had been married, and she'd had three sons.

"Mrs. Jane Watmore. Married to a man by the name of Carlson Watmore. Sons were, in order of birth, Carlson Jr., Phillip, and then Trevor. Trevor, we think, might have died soon after birth. There is the payment of a headstone here." He had called Lauren, who was just as excited as he was.

128

"Also, there is mention of a woman, but nothing other than her initials, that might have been a servant here, as well as a good friend of Jane's. WB is all I know about her."

"Okay, and you think they might have served in the military?" He said that it looked as if they might have been killed, and she had two telegrams from them. "Okay, that narrows it down, because they should have dates as well as their ID numbers on them."

He read those off to her as well. "I only want to find out if there are any survivors of this family. We've found some things in the house and outbuildings that someone might want." Lauren said that she understood that. "Let me know if you find anything, and whatever it is. Also, the sister, I nearly forgot her. Her name was Marie Ross. There is nothing more on her that we've been able to find."

"This is good. It'll take me a couple of hours to get something back to you. However, if you find something else, just let me know. I like getting my teeth into stuff like this. Also, there are some things you might want to consider before contacting them. If there are children and they weren't notified, they might need something more than trinkets. They might want your house. I'd look into that too. People suck, as you know." He said that he'd look into it. "As for your business, you've been cleared of any and all wrong doings, so you can open back up if you wish."

"I'm not sure." Lauren said she understood that as well. "Yes, well, maybe I'll just work from home and be choosy about who I work with. I can't do that anymore and be happy about it. Besides, I love being a house husband." She pointed out that Colin had too. "Yes, but he had four little ones underfoot. That would scare even the most sainted man."

When he hung up after giving her all the information

129

that he could, Larson helped his dad take some of the bigger pieces in the house. There was indeed a cabinet to put the dishes in, as well as a sideboard and a couple of old frames that matched it all. As he was setting the cabinet in the corner, where it would be moved to, he stepped back to have a look at it.

"You thinking that you want it there?" He looked at Dad and asked him where he'd put it. "I was thinking over in the other corner, that way when we bring in the table there will be more room."

Before he could move it again by wrapping his arms around it, a piece of the wood popped open. Standing back, he looked inside the small compartment and saw something there. Pulling the entire piece out, he laid it on the wire roll that was being used. It was full of jewelry and small stones.

"Well I'll be dog napped and put to sleep." Larson looked at his dad and thought him the strangest man he'd ever known when it came to being surprised about things. "You thinking that she hid it in there to keep her sister from finding it? I heard tell that the woman, the sister, she wasn't a peach."

There was a pair of earrings that looked to be rubies, very old ones if the color was any indication. A wedding ring with diamonds surrounding it, as well as several smaller diamonds in a black bag and a couple of other stones that he wasn't sure of. Larson wasn't sure what to do with them.

"I'd just be making a list of what you find and where you found it. That way, you got yourself covered in case someone comes looking for it." He told his dad what he'd been told about the house from the bank. "Yeah, you do get whatever you find, but that don't mean that people won't be wanting a piece of it."

That was true. So, as he made a list of things that they

had unearthed, he took pictures of them and sent them to his computer. Larson decided to make a file and have it ready should Lauren find anyone that might come back on them.

The rest of the afternoon was spent bringing in other pieces that his dad had deemed worthy of his rooms. It was funny really, the way his dad had wrapped each piece up with care and told the movers that they had to be extra careful with them. He told him later that these were part of history, something that you just couldn't go back and make again. Dad pointed out the craftsmanship of the large sideboard they'd brought in, and told him how the wood wasn't even around any longer.

Larson found Virginia in her office working with Sam in the little bed beside her. Not bothering either of them, he brought in more boxes to be gone through, as well as some more crates. At the rate they were going, it would be years before they got around to getting everything emptied. Not that he cared…he was having a blast, and he was sure his dad was too.

When he was called to dinner by Flo, he hadn't any idea that she'd come back, he'd been so involved with what he was doing. She told him that her things would be delivered tomorrow sometime, and asked if he'd help her get them set up.

"Anything you need, I'm there for you." He looked at the doorway and saw the table was still empty. "Should we go and get Virginia and Sam?"

"No, not unless you want to have her upset. When she's writing a new book, it's easier just to drop off food for her and clean up when she's done. And remind her, gently, to go to bed." He laughed when she did. "I swear to you, Larson, she'll be fine. It's how she does it, and it works for her, so she doesn't change. I keep an eye on her. I love doing it for you both."

"Thank you. I guess I can understand that. I like my own space and how I do things as well. How long do you think she'll be under?"

They were both laughing when Virginia entered the dining room. After he asked how she was, she sat down beside him at the table.

"It's the strangest thing. I was working away when I suddenly had a need to find you and come to eat. I've never done that before." Larson told Virginia that he was glad that she had, and what he'd been doing today. "Do you need for me to help you?"

"No, not unless you want to. I have it under control. You do your thing and I'll do mine. I think that works for us both, don't you?" She nodded and grinned at him.

They were both laughing when Lauren came in the room. He could tell that she'd had some success with looking up the names, and when she handed him a thick file, he looked up at her and asked if it was bad.

"Bad? No, I don't think so, but there is a lot of information that you should have. And when you've read that, I want you to come see me. I have something I want to do, and you have to be involved." He told her anything. "Good, I was hoping you'd say that. The bodies of the three sons are buried someplace on this property. I'd like to find them and take them to someplace special. They were good men, and one was a mere child."

~~~

Carl looked over the letter again. He'd been called to an attorney's office earlier this morning, and had dropped everything to come and see what was befalling him again.

Since he'd not been doing anything anyway, it had been easy for him to *drop* things to come in. Being out of work was hurting him badly right now.

"I don't understand this. It says that they want to exhume my long dead grandfather and bury him someplace else? I thought that he was lost overseas." He rubbed his forehead and looked at the name of the person sending this. "Is this a joke? The President of the United States contacted you?"

"Yes sir, he did. And I got on the first plane I could to come and let you know his plans. What is it you know about your long dead relatives?" Carl told him next to nothing, as his father was a bastard child. "I see. Well, the estate was settled some time ago, and the house, your family home, was sold. But the family that purchased it, they found some things in the house that they think might belong to you."

"If they found some unpaid bills, then I'm afraid they're going to be out of luck with that. I can barely make it now." He assured him that there were no bills. "Then what is it they think I'd want? I mean, I've not had anything to do with the Watmores since...well, I've never had anything to do with them. My father didn't know much about them even before his mom told him who they were."

"We have a record of your grandfather and his brothers. He and one brother were good soldiers—the other brother died as a child—and your grandfather, Carlson Jr., was killed before your father was born. We've talked to a few people that might have some information, and they say that if he had known about your dad, he would have married your grandmother and made arrangements to have them brought to his family home." Carl said that was all well and good, but a bit too late. "You might be wrong about that, sir. The family, as I said, they have some things that you might want."

133

"Did they say what?" He said that he didn't know, but they wanted to see him. "Is this a scam? I mean, it's nice of them if it's all true, but I've seen enough on the television to know that this sort of thing, scams like this, happen all the time. I don't want to sound ungrateful, but I just don't think I could handle any more bad shit coming my way."

"I don't blame you, sir. But I assure you, this is all on the up and up. The McCullough family is an upstanding one. And if they say they want you to come and see what they've found, they think it will be worth your time." He nodded. What did he have to lose, really? "There is a plane for you to use, and housing has been set up for you as well. A number of people would like to talk to you, once you have settled whatever you need to at the house. All right?"

"And you're sure this isn't a way to get me there for something terrible? I don't usually have this sort of thing happen to me. I mean, just bill collectors and such." Again, he assured him that it was legitimate. "All right. I can go out there, but I have to warn you, if this is a scam, I'm not going to be able to come back here and face the fact that I have ten days to clear out of my home and move on. On to where I have no idea, but my life is falling apart around me."

The next morning he was on a plane on his way to Ohio. To say that he'd been surprised by the private jet sitting on the tarmac just for him would have been a gross understatement. As he was asked if he needed anything, water or food, Carl wondered at the expense of this venture. If it was a scam, which he was beginning to believe it wasn't, then it was a very costly one for someone.

A limo was waiting when he landed. Carl wasn't so naive that he thought this was normal for anyone. As he was driven to the hotel or wherever he was staying, he thought about the kind of money it would take to just do the simple things that had been done for him. Not only had he been flown here and put up, but he'd been given a gift card of a thousand dollars to help him along the way.

As soon as the limo stopped, he sat there and stared at the huge house he was in front of.

"Hello, you must be Carl Watmore." He nodded at the woman. "I'm Lauren McCullough. I'm so glad that you decided to come and stay with us a few days. For however long you wish, really. We have a lot to talk about."

"I don't know what's going on." She said that she'd explain it to him. "I hope so. I can't help with anything on the family, I'm afraid. My dad, he knew nothing of them, and when I came along late in their life, my mom passed away and then he did a few months later. I've been alone for a long time, Ms. McCullough."

"You're not anymore." He nodded and followed her into the house. "We've found out that your great uncles, both of them, didn't have any children. Trevor was an infant when he passed away...from diphtheria, we think." She continued talking as they entered the big house. "Your great uncle Phillip was an infantry man in the Army, and did a lot of things that should have earned him the Medal of Honor. However, he wasn't given that because when his body was to be interred into the cemetery, it was lost. And that of your grandfather."

"Lost? How does the Army lose a body?" They were in a large office, and the walls were covered in pictures with sticky notes attached to them. He walked to the first one he recognized and asked if that was his father. "I mean, he looks like him, but this picture, it's very old, isn't it?"

"Yes. That's your great grandfather. And the one below it is your father. He was born about seven months after his father was killed. We think it might have been a month or so before his death was recognized, but it's hard to gauge it exactly since it was war time." He nodded and looked at the other photos before turning back to Ms. McCullough. "You're the last of your family, Mr. Watmore. None of the others had children, and even before that, there were few children born to the family that lived. We'd like for you to see some of the things that were found in the family home. It might explain a few things to you."

"Why?" She asked him what he meant. "Why does anyone care about this? Or me, for that matter? I'm a man on the verge of losing everything I have, which really isn't all that much anyway. I have no money, no ties to this place, and I don't know any of them. As I said to that attorney, I never knew a thing about any of them."

"Yes, we're aware of that, but as I said, you're their only living relative, and being such, you are entitled to all that would have come to them, had we known about your dad." He asked her what that meant. "Backpay, sir. You are entitled not only to the back pay as a descendant of your father, but also some benefits that we've made sure you can take advantage of. Your father, had the Army known about him, would have been on the receiving end of this, but you are now in line to get them."

He was getting too much too fast. When he sat down on the little chair in the office, he put his head between his knees. Not that he was sick, but he had to close out some of the bombardment of words and information coming his way. When he saw the shoes of a man in front of him, he started to raise his head and wasn't able to.

"I don't want you to freak out when you see me." He said he was all right now. "Yes, but my presence has an effect on people that makes me want to cringe. Remember, Mr. Watmore, I'm just a man."

He lifted his head when the hand was moved. Carl nearly put it back down between his knees when he realized who was there. The president smiled at him, and Carl felt himself smiling back. Carl leaned back in his chair when the president sat down too.

"My friend, Lauren, has gone to a lot of trouble to find you, sir. I'd hate to have to explain to her that I scared you so badly that you ran away." Carl told him he was in a dream. "No, I'm here and I'm real. There are times, even now, that I find it hard to believe myself that I'm president, but I'd like for you to call me Jarvis."

"Like we're friends?" He lowered his voice a little, embarrassed that he'd squeaked. "I'm sorry, I'm trying to wrap my head around all this."

"It is a lot to take in, but if you can stand a little more, I'd like to thank you and your family for your loyalty and service to our country." Carl nodded and told him he didn't know them. "That's what I'm doing here. I want you to know that you're not going to endure any costs for what I'm about to tell you. We want to bury your relatives in a place of honor. And how they disappeared is something that I'm sure happened a great deal back then, but their bodies were shipped home rather than through the normal routes. I'm sorry."

Carl nodded, still not sure what he was supposed to be doing here. Yes, he supposed they were his family by some fluke. He supposed that in some way, all this about his dad's birth and the way he'd been left alone might be just the way he'd said, but there were other things going on that he wasn't sure how he was involved.

"We would like for you to come with us when we honor

them." He asked where. "Arlington. They should have been buried there, along with their comrades, in a place of honor."

"My great grandmother…is she in trouble for this? I mean, I know that she's long gone, but I'd hate to have someone tarnish her name now that it's been found out." Jarvis laughed a little. "I don't know what I should be thinking."

"Your great grandmother won't have her name tarnished. From what we've been able to piece together, she lost more than most when she sent her boys to war. She lost her husband early in their marriage and was left alone to grieve. Ms. Watmore became a recluse for a long time, and didn't open her home for many years. It was the talk of the town, I guess." He nodded, realizing that he had a lot in common with the elder woman. "When she died, her sister, a terrible woman from our information, came here and took over the family home. Not that it was hers, but she did it anyway, tearing out anything that had belonged to her sister and putting it in storage. That's how we found out about the children, as well as you."

"And what does that mean, exactly?" Jarvis smiled. "I don't know you well, sir, but I don't think that's going to bode well for me. What's going on? I can take it."

"Come with me and we'll show you what we've found, and you can decide what you want to do. The McCulloughs own the house and all the contents, so you keep that in mind when you meet them. What they're doing, it's above and beyond what others would do for a stranger." He nodded. "Larson and Virginia are newly married too, so getting their attention might be a bit hard."

They might have a hard time, but he thought he was well beyond having a hard time paying attention. This all had come out of the blue for him, and he felt like he was on one of those rides at the county fair. The one that would shake you up and let you try and stand on your own. He felt just like that.

Chapter 10

Larson was nervous. Not just nervous, but also excited. He had everything laid out for the man, including some of the love letters that they'd found. He looked at Virginia when she joined him in the library.

Carl had arrived two days ago, and had been shown the town and taken to lunch and dinner by at least half the family. The other half of them had been telling him what was found, showing him around and having a good time with him. He was a very nice and gentle man. He'd even had a few conversations with him since he'd gotten here.

"Are you ready for this?" He nodded, then shook his head. "Yeah, right there with you on that one. I have no idea what to expect, but I'm excited and afraid at the same time. What do you suppose he'll want to do with the things we've found for him?"

"I don't know. Lauren said that he's broke, and that even coming here has set him back a few bucks. I guess he's been afraid to use the credit card she gave him for fear it was fake too." Virginia told him she could understand that. "I guess

141

you would. You told me that you and your mom lived in your car for a time. My family has always had money, but we never spent it like we did. We had chores, and got allowances when we did them. My parents had rules and we were made to follow them."

"My mom had rules too, but it was hard to enforce them when there was nothing to take from me. Not that I was a rule breaker. I knew that we were poor and helped anyway I could. Now that I have money coming in from my books, I do find that I want to make sure she has it all because she has given up so much for me. But I would imagine that most kids would be that way." He didn't think so but said nothing. "Oh, Jon is here. He said he'd talk to the man if he thought he might need it, but wasn't worried about him. And we're not to rush him too much, but he mentioned that he's nearly out of time. I don't know what that means really, but Lauren told me and she likes her rules followed as well. She said that he's overwhelmed, too."

The workers in the house had been given the day off. It wasn't close to being done, but they did have the kitchen, living room, and the dining room complete. Also, Virginia's and his office was nearly done. That, to him, was the best part.

He loved his new office and all the beautiful antiques that they'd found to fill it with. Some of the things that Virginia had had at her other home had arrived the other day, and they'd donated most of it to the local project that stored things like that for when there was a fire or someone lost everything in other ways.

When the front door was opened, Larson counted to ten before going into the hall. They had staff now, just a few people to help them out with the house, but it was something that they both had to get used to. As soon as he saw the older man, he knew just how he felt. Overwhelmed, stressed, and unsure.

"Hello, Mr. Watmore. I'm so glad that you could come to our house today. Meeting in town has been nice, but this is your family home." He shook his hand and then Virginia's. Instead of going to the dining room, she led them to the living room. "My wife and I, we've been digging through your history, as you know, and wanted to share it with you. I know it's a little late to ask, but we've also dug around in your past as well. And we'd like to help you."

"Help me? And if you've looked even a little into my life, Mr. McCullough, you know that I have nothing. Not even a home by the time I get back." Larson nodded and asked him to have a seat. "My family, you said they lived here at one time?"

"Yes, all of them did, and they're buried here as well. Not your father, though we can take care that he is as well if you'd like, along with your mom. We only just found the little cemetery about a week ago. Well, we found it before then, but we've only just figured out who is buried there." He nodded and took a cup of tea when it was offered to him. "My wife and I would like to help you out with your life, if you'd allow us to. And I'm to understand that you have some money coming your way from the government as well."

"That's what I've been told too." Carl looked around the room, and so did Larson. "I have never lived in a house. Grand or otherwise. A home for the most part that had about a dozen or so other kids in it. Then trailers for the rest of the time. I'm not telling you this to make you feel sorry for me, just telling you. But this is very nice. I really love what you've done so far."

"It's been a huge undertaking, getting this house back to

livable. It was left with no regard to what happened to the things left behind. We've discovered a great many things about the people who lived here." He showed him the fireplace, and pointed out that the mantel and some of the bricks had had to be replaced. "We've decided, since there are gas lines to the house, that we'd make this a gas fireplace. We're modernizing a lot of things here. Your family, they might well have been happy with the changes, I think."

"My relatives." Larson nodded, and that was when Jon joined them. He didn't say anything, but joined them on the couch. Carl sat in the wingback that had only just come back from being redone. "As I've said, several times now, I don't know any of them. My parents died when I was young, almost too young to remember them. I've been nearly on the verge of losing everything since I struck out on my own at sixteen. Whatever you need or think you might need from me, I don't think I can help you."

"We know that." He nodded and set the cup down, half finished. "Your family was very wealthy. So much so that they didn't care about the cost of things, and it's doubtful if they ever thought of anything beyond getting what they wanted. Not that they were rude people, but they did have money and didn't care how they spent it." He asked him if he knew how much. "Yes. When your grandfather went off to war, the family was worth about two million. By today's standards, that isn't a great deal of money. But then, they were wealthy beyond anyone around."

"I think two million is a great deal of money. I have about two bucks to my name." Larson felt his face heat up and told him he was sorry, he'd not meant to belittle him. "You didn't. I'm just telling you the facts."

"Among the things that we found, there is a policy that

144

hasn't been cashed in, as well as some gemstones and other things. Things that we'd like to give you." He asked him why. "Because they're a part of your family."

"Mr. McCullough, I know that you're married. You have a lovely home, one that I don't know. You have family right here, all around you all the time. Do you have children?" He told him that they had one that they'd recently adopted, and his wife was expecting their second child. "Family. I don't have that. Not even the makings of one. I don't have children to pass any of this down to. I have nowhere, as of now, to store such things if I were to take them."

Larson started to explain to him that it belonged to him when Virginia spoke. She had been quiet until then. Jon winked at him when she sounded pissed off, something that he was afraid was going to make it worse for the poor man.

"Oh, for Christ's sake. Just shut up and listen, will you? We have an insurance policy that was found that is worth just over a hundred thousand dollars. Your great grandmother might have been a little nuts and rude, but she knew to take care of her family. I do know that she knew about your dad, and tried to find him well after the war was over. We might not ever know to what levels she tried, but she took out this policy for any family that came forward when she died. That would have been her sister, I suppose, and let me tell you, that woman was a fucking bitch by all accounts. But she didn't find it, and even went so far as to make this place in her image. She's who we have to thank for having so much shit to sort through. But in a way, I'm glad that she took it upon herself to tear out the old and put in what would have been new back them. Because the treasures we've found are going to keep us happy for a long time." She stood up and handed him the box that they'd found just last night. "Those are pictures of

145

your relatives long past. He was a handsome man, and loved your grandmother. He wrote more letters home about your grandmotherher than most people do in several lifetimes. But he was killed before he could bring her home to meet his mom, and she never was able to find her. And she looked."

Larson watched as Carl opened the box with trembling hands. He had seen the pictures, all of them older than he was by nearly three times. There were pictures not only of Carl Jr., but his parents, Jane and Carlson Sr., as well as the other family members. There was even a tintype of the younger brother when he was in his casket. A morbid picture, but history all the same.

"These are...I've never known any of them, not even to know their names." He was teary and Larson felt bad for him. "My dad always joked about being the son of a rich man. He wasn't around for very long after I was about four or five. But that was how he explained to me why I had no grandparents to go visit when the other kids around me did."

"Jane looked for her for decades, it seems. All she knew about your grandmother was that she had been a war baby, and that her parents were gone by the time that Carl Jr. had fallen in love with her. When he was killed, she received all his letters from her, and even with the address, it was nearly impossible to find her. But with today's technology, not only were we able to find her, but where her parents are buried as well." Carl thanked them for the pictures, then looked at Virginia. "We've made arrangements for you to stay with us for the rest of your stay, if you would. We'd like to show you what we've found out about your family, and give you more than just a pot to piss in, as my mom is fond of saying."

"I don't know what to say." She told him that he didn't need to say anything, just to say yes. "Yes, I'd like that. But

146

I need to find some work, if there is any to be had. I'll need money to get around with."

"The policy that we told you about is at the bank. All you need to do is sign it and you'll have all the cash you need while here. But I'm hoping that you'll stay here. To live around here." He said he'd have to think on that, then told her he'd like that as well. "Good. I'm glad to hear that. Come on, we have to get things set up for you. And if you don't mind, we'll have you sign off on moving your family around a little bit. Your uncle and grandfather are war heroes, and they need to be someplace so they can be honored."

He signed off on the paperwork and then was taken to the barn. Larson was so excited that he nearly forgot about Jon. When he pulled him aside, Larson asked him if things were all right.

"Yes, but he isn't kidding when he tells you that he's broke. I know that you knew that, but he's also very ill and cannot afford to see a doctor about it." Larson asked him what was wrong with him. "Cancer. He is riddled with it now. There is no hope for him, but for my blood. I can help him, if you wish. I won't mind, and I think he's deserving, don't you?"

"Yes. I don't know why, but if that's what you think, then I'm all right with that." Jon nodded. "What else? I can tell there is something else that you want to tell me."

"Yes, there is. But it can wait. You should spend as much time with him as you can. He's a nice man, but he really is dying. He is aware of this, but he doesn't have long to live." Larson asked him how soon. "You and Aunt Virginia have extended things for him, simply by being who you are, but he'll never spend the money that you are giving him in the form of the policy, nor will he live long enough to see his family buried again."

Larson didn't want to think of the elderly man dying. He'd only just met him, and didn't want him to leave so soon. But they would make life easier for him, in any way possible. As soon as he saw him with Flo, Larson looked at Jon again when he touched his hand to his shoulder.

"He will find love." Larson asked him what he meant. "Flo. Not the same, but she is his mate. And I will make it so that they can be happy, if that's what you want too. But you must explain things to him, today if you can. Flo is his other half."

"Really?" Jon said that he was telling him the truth. "I know that, but for them both to need someone and finding it so close to us, it's wonderful, don't you think?"

"Yes. But I won't help him until he understands what I can do for him." Larson said he'd do it, today. "Hurry, Uncle Larson. He really doesn't have that long to live."

~~~

Virginia wasn't sure that the man understood what was going to happen. He seemed as lost as any soul she'd ever seen. Mom was holding his hand, something that she was surprised by until Larson explained. They were mates, or something like that. And Jon could save his life.

"You mean, all I need to do is drink a little of his blood and I'll be fine? I have to tell you, young man, I've been sick for some time, and if you're just saying this to give me a little happiness before I die, then I don't think that's very nice of you." Larson said that he'd never lie about something like this. "Yes, I'm sure that you wouldn't, but you have and I don't like it."

"Do you believe in shifters, Carl? I mean, have you seen them? Been around them?" He said that he had. "I'm a cat...a jaguar, as a matter of fact. My nephew Jon, he's a little of

148

everything. And can do more things with just his hand than even an elite shifter can do. He has saved all our lives over the months he's been here, and will continue to do so. And he can save your life. As I said, you don't have much time, and he wants you to understand what will be involved if you let him help you."

"And this nice lady here, she's going to love me, no matter what? I suppose she's been helped by this young man too?" She had, as a matter of fact, and it wasn't until Mom stood up that Virginia knew what it was going to take for him to believe. "I'm sorry, I just don't want to be sucked into this. I'm a dying man."

"Yes, you are." Mom walked to her and nodded as she continued. "Darling, will you please try and kill your mother? I don't want to have to find love for the first time in my life, then have it taken away by something as nasty as cancer."

"Mom, I can't do that." She said that she could and should. "No. I'm not going to try and take your life. Even though I know that you can live through it, my heart would break for doing such a thing to you. I can't do that."

Mom looked at Jon and he nodded. "Will you forgive me, Grandma?" She nodded then hugged Jon. He smiled gently at her as he held her to him and stabbed her twice in the back. When Virginia started for them, Larson stopped her.

"I love you all so very much."

The blood was real and plentiful, but her mom only smiled at her. When she lifted her shirt up and showed Carl the wounds that had all but sealed, Mom took him by the hand and told him that was what Jon's blood could do for him.

Jon walked toward him then and put out his hand to Carl. He was still staring at the wounds that had disappeared

149

when he was stood up. Jon said his name three times before he finally looked at him.

"I can save your life. But you have to understand that you'll live forever." He nodded, and Virginia wasn't sure he was understanding this. "Forever, Carl. Do you understand that? And you'll have magic of your own to call on."

"You knew she wasn't going to die when you did that, didn't you?" Jon said that he knew it. "And this thing you want to do to me, it'll give me that? The ability to live a long time and not hurt anymore? Boy, I have to tell you, I hurt like the dickens all the time."

"I assure you, Carl, you'll no longer hurt, nor will you die. That's important that you know that. You won't die." Carl repeated what he said, and Virginia still wasn't sure he fully understood. But she knew that not hurting anymore would be something that he'd focus on. "Are you ready? As much as I'd like to give you time, you don't have a great deal of it left, do you?"

"No. I probably would be dead now had I not had this trip to look forward to. I mean, I thought it was a sham. Even up to the point where the limo picked me up at the airport. But I wanted so badly for it to be true. That someone out there knew who I was and where I came from. I want you to save me, young man. And if you say that I'm going to be getting to love this woman here, then I'm all for that too." Jon nodded and hugged him. "You're a good family. I'm so glad that you called me. So, if this doesn't work, I'm beholden to you for even trying."

"It will work. All you need to do is drink a little of my blood." Carl looked around the room and all of them nodded. "That's all there is to it. You might feel a little dizzy afterwards, but you'll be as good as new."

"All right then, let's get it going." Carl held her mom's hand then kissed the back of it. "You sure are a beautiful woman, Flo. I do hope this works for us. I'd love to be your other half."

It had only taken a small drop for them, but with Carl being so ill and so close to his own death, she thought it should take a little more. When Jon cut his finger, just on the tip, she watched as the tiny droplets landed on the other man's tongue. She counted seven, and then looked at her mom.

"You'll need just a bit more, I think." She knew then that the doctor's visit that her mom had gone to yesterday hadn't been all that normal. "You need to speak to your daughter too, Grandma Flo."

"Yes, I will." The drops on her mom's tongue were two, but she was worried now. And as soon as her mom hugged her, she asked her what was going on. "They found a tiny lump. Nothing much, they told me, but it worried me, you know. To live a very long time and to be ill the entire time wouldn't be very good, don't you think? But I was going to talk to you when I got the results back. I promise you."

"Don't keep things from me, please? I need to know that you're all right and that you're going to be around for the rest of my life." She hugged her and whispered in her ear. "I'm going to have a baby. I was going to wait too, until I knew for sure, but Larson said it was true, and I have no reason not to believe him."

They were going out to the barn when Carl suddenly stopped moving. Mom rushed to him and asked him several times if he was all right. But all he did was stare straight ahead. Virginia looked too, trying to see what had startled him, but she saw nothing. Then Carl fell to his knees and she began to worry more.

"It's the magic. It's healing him." Virginia looked at Jon when he spoke quietly. "By the end of today, he would have died in his sleep. Had he been at his home, they would have found him weeks later, his body left in the house for no one to find that loved him. We've given him not just a second chance, but a life too."

"Will he be all right?" He nodded as Larson picked Carl up and carried him to the side entrance to the house, where her mom was living. Mom was right behind them. "He'll be all right, won't he?"

"Yes. He'll need rest. A great deal of it. And time to get used to his new energy and life. I don't know, to be honest with you, how he has made it this far. The man was eaten up with cancer." Virginia sat down on the bench and Jon asked her if she was all right too.

"I'm fine. Nervous, I guess. And scared a little." He grinned at her. "How do you know all this stuff, Jon? I mean, I know that you're special and all, but you seem to know a great deal about everyone. Does it ever get to you? Knowing the outcome before it happens?"

He sat with her. "Sometimes. I don't care for some of the things I've been able to see. And I do have trouble at times remembering that some of the things I've seen haven't happened yet, and I must keep it straight. I have seen your child." She stared at him. "Would you like to know anything about it? Sex? Or even what it gets from you as a cat?"

"No. I don't think I want to know. I mean, knowing that I'm having a baby is really wonderful, and having a child by the man that I love makes it even better. But I think knowing too much would just be that, too much." He nodded as if he understood what she was saying. "Jon, I don't really want to know much about my future. I mean, if it's my child or with this family, then tell me, but my own? I think I'd like to do that as it comes. Does that make sense to you?"

"It does. You want to be unaware of things. Feel them when they happen. I love that. I can't see my own future, not clearly. But, and this is only since coming here, I'm very glad that I've been a part of this family. You will find none better when it comes to loving and protecting you, as they have me a great deal."

"And you have them as well, I believe." He nodded and stood up, telling her that he had things to take care of. "Be careful please. I know that you're this all-powerful being, but I also know that you can be hurt. Don't let anyone harm you, Jon."

When he wandered off, she made her way to the barn. There were a few things in there that she wanted to get cleaned up. A cradle that had been handmade by someone with loving hands, as well as the rocker. She was sad to see that both items were missing. Virginia went back to the house and checked on Carl.

"He'll sleep for a few hours, then when he wakes, he'll be hungry." Mom nodded at Boyd as he put his things back in his bag. "I'd say start with some broth, but I'm thinking he'll want food…steaks and potatoes. Can you do that for him?"

"Absolutely. I'd enjoy it." Mom turned and looked at her. "You leave him to me, and I'll have him up and around in no time."

"See that you do." She and Larson left with Boyd and made their way to the second level of the house. Stretching out on the couch, she tuned out the brothers and closed her eyes. Exhaustion was never far from her nowadays, and she usually let it take her. Today was no exception.

Chapter 11

Thanksgiving was in two days, and Larson was looking forward to it more than any of the others they'd had as a family. He had one this time, a wife, a son, and one on the way. Life to him was pretty perfect. And his mom had asked him to have the dinner this year when the house came along much faster than anyone would have thought. She asked simply because his house was big enough to accommodate their growing family.

"I've ordered the turkey and it'll be here in the morning." Larson thanked Ben, their cook. "Also, there are a few bottles of wine in the cellar that we've been able to bring up here that I thought would be a nice touch."

"Excellent idea. How much of that stuff down there have you been able to catalog? I guess it's taking you a little longer than you thought." He said that he'd found yet another room filled with the bottles. "When the ladies were here yesterday, putting in the last of the mulch, they told me they thought there was a grape arbor around here at one time. In the spring, we're going to have to have a look for it."

155

"I believe I might have heard that as well." He stood there and Larson waited. The man was an excellent cook, but he was a little shy about asking for things he might need. "I was wondering something, sir. If you say no, then I will completely understand. But with all the work going on around here being almost finished, I was wondering if we could see about expanding the cook's quarters for myself and my wife."

"There are cook's quarters?" Larson knew there were. He'd had them worked on too. "Show me. I had no idea that there was a part of the house that I'd not had a look at."

It had been planned for a few days now that they surprise the man with the living arrangements. His wife was in on the plan, and had told him just that morning that she was going to beg him to ask Larson. So, as they headed up the stairs to the rooms for them, he asked him how he'd found them.

"They were on the plans that you've hung in the library. I had a looksee at them when we first arrived. They're a mess, sir. So, if it's too expensive to have it fixed up enough so that we can stay over some nights when you're working late, I fully understand."

Larson didn't say anything, but did laugh when he went on about the cost. "Ben, you do know that my wife is a famous author, don't you? And that she keeps me in money. Not that we need either of us to work, but we're able to afford to have a room or two spruced up for you." Ben thanked him. "This is it? Seems a lot of dark halls, don't you think?"

"Oh, but it only needs a coat or two of paint and a little rug here and there. But the rooms, they're behind this door." He nodded to him to open them. "Yes, of course. Just this way."

As soon as the door was opened, everyone yelled surprise. His family was there, as well as Ben's wife and two children. They'd been flown in for just this occasion. There were a couple of grandchildren there as well, and Larson was glad that Virginia had thought of having them stay for the holidays too.

"Oh my." Larson patted the man on the back as he gave him a little push into the rooms. "You knew about this? You knew that I was going to ask you?"

"I did. And it was our pleasure to have it happen for you and your wife." Virginia joined him and Ben as he continued. "There are some pieces of furniture here that were up in this part of the house when we started on it. So, if there are things that you don't want or need, let me know and we'll take them out. Your furniture is here as well. Set up the way your lovely wife wanted it done."

He was shown around the apartment-like setting after he greeted his family. Ben carried one of his grandsons with him as he went from room to room, telling the little boy that he'd have room for him to stay should he wish it. As they made their way to the living room again, Ben hugged him several times as he thanked him for such a fine gift.

"You're so very welcome. And your family will be joining us for Thanksgiving, as will you and your wife. My mom has called in some help to make things happen so that you will sit with us and be thankful." He said he couldn't do that. "Well, then you have to talk to Lauren."

"Oh no. No, no, no. I shall have a meal with you. I'm deathly afraid of Ms. Lauren. She is very stern, don't you think?" He laughed and told him that he was afraid of her as well. And had to tell Lauren that her idea had worked like a charm to get him to have dinner with them.

Leaving Ben's family to talk, his family came to the kitchen with him and Virginia. He wanted them all to go away, but knew that it would be considered rude to run them off when they were his family. Instead, he pulled out the sandwiches that had been brought for lunch, and they sat around the dining room table being family for a while.

"I've been thinking about the office that you have downtown. I want to buy it." He asked his dad why. "I've got me a hankering to have myself a little place I can go and do some stuff. Stuff for myself."

"I see." Mom smacked him on the shoulder, and Larson laughed as he continued to query his dad. "And this stuff that you want to do, does it have anything to do with the woodworking equipment that has already been delivered there? Or perhaps the work that is being done to upgrade the electrical circuits that are in there?"

"Dab nabbit boy, can't a man have anything done without everybody snooping around in it?" He told his dad that he had to sign for it. "Oh. Never thought of that. Anyhoo. I want to buy that building off of you. I do want to figure out if I can make some of the pretty work we have to send out. I got me a lot of time now to learn it, and I want to have a go at it."

"You can have it, Dad. Anything that you want. You've worked really hard on this house, and I love every part of it. I could not have asked for better craftsmanship on any of this." His dad flustered about how he'd had a lot of help, and that he'd only done a bit of it. Larson knew better. "It's wonderful, and the building is yours if you want it. I've already had it cleared of the things I wanted. You can even have the computer and printer that's there as well."

They talked about the upcoming holidays, the fact that there were so many of them now, and Mom was excited. It was like all the times when they'd been children and living at home. A lot of talking, but not much accomplished. And they

158

were loud. He loved every second of it.

When they left, he sat in the living room. This was the only room where they'd had to buy furniture so far. A mattress here and there, and maybe a safer lamp, but in this room they'd had to start from scratch, and he was happy with the results. Virginia joined him a few minutes later and sat near him on the long sofa.

"I went to the barn to get the baby cradle and the rocking chair, and they're gone. I guess your dad had other uses for them." Larson didn't say anything, knowing that his parents were having them both redone for Virginia for Christmas. She laid her head on his chest. "Larson, is it going to be okay with having my mom and her—well, I don't know what to call him…my step-dad, I guess—living in the basement?"

"Of course. Anything that makes your mom happy, makes us happy. Right?" She nodded and yawned for the second time in as many minutes. "The dinner arrangements are finished, Mom told me. She said that other than the turkey to go in the oven first thing and the other things heated up, we're finished."

"Reese is making some pies and cakes too." Her yawning had him yawning too. "I'm so tired lately. I haven't been sleeping well either. I think it's the deadline that I'm up against. I know that I should go work, but I don't have the energy. If I take a little nap, maybe I can work later."

"You do that, love. And I'll hold you." He was dozing himself when he heard the front door open. His family didn't knock unless they were sure you had company. He didn't either when he went to their homes. And no one ever knocked on his parents' door. That's how you knew when there were strangers around.

He looked over his shoulders at the young man standing

there. He looked lost. More than that, he looked to be starving. Larson had no idea how he knew he was like Jon, but he nodded to him and quietly asked him to have a seat. He did so without any hesitation. That was when he noticed the blood.

"I'm assuming that's not yours." He looked down at his hands as if he'd never seen them before. "My name is Larson McCullough. This is my wife, Virginia." He woke her up and before she could speak, he nodded to the young man. "He just came in the house."

"Hello." He nodded at Virginia. "You must be Jon's friend. He's around here somewhere. He told me the other day that someone was coming. Did you talk to him?"

"We can talk, but I don't much. It'll get us caught. The blood is mine. I hurt myself getting away this time." Larson asked him if he was followed. "No. I changed into something they couldn't trace and came here after a couple of days. They hurt me with something."

"Larson, please ask Jon to join us. I'm going to get this young man some dinner." She was being very casual, and he was worried about that. As they left the room, he contacted Jon to let him know what was going on.

I'm on my way. I meant to talk to you about it as well, but I kept getting busy on other things. His name is...well, he doesn't have one. Much like I didn't when I came here. He asked him if he was in trouble. *Yes, we all are at some point. But he's smart enough not to get anyone else hurt too.* He told me that he was being extra careful not to be followed.

Virginia is feeding him now. He was covered in blood when he arrived. I'm assuming, like you, he heals when he's full. He said that he thought so. *Jon, why my house? Not that I care, but he ended up here.*

To divert anyone thinking that we're the same. If he would have

160

come to my home, with my parents, they might start thinking about the fact that I have shown up. He said he'd never thought of that. *We all need to think like criminals. Lauren told me that. It's scary the way her mind works, isn't it?*

Yes. He asked him where he was. He told him. *In the tree behind the house? Why not just come in the house and talk to him?*

Because he isn't there. Larson felt his heartrate triple. *Uncle Larson, that man, he's not T-2. You must get to Aunt Virginia.*

He came around the corner to the kitchen area, and was confronted by the young man holding Virginia in front of him. He had a gun to her head and was talking, but nothing that he could understand.

"He wants you to let me go with him. Larson, if you let this bastard hurt you, I'm going to be really upset with you. He's a liar and a thief. He wants me to give him my wedding bands." He told her it was better than her getting hurt. "It most certainly is not. I love these. Kick his ass for me."

"I'm going to, honey, but we need to talk to him first. He has a big gun to your head." She stomped her foot, and if this wasn't so serious he might have laughed at her. "Jon is here. He is calling my brothers."

The little mouse that entered the hallway with them stood on his hind legs and waved at him. Again, the urge to laugh was painful to keep hidden, but he knew that Jon was only telling him it was him and not a random rodent.

"What do you think you're going to accomplish by coming into my home and taking my wife hostage?" He said he wanted money. "Sadly, so does the rest of the world, and they're not any closer to getting it than you are. Let her go and I won't have to hurt you."

"Where is this Jon kid? Maybe he has some on him." The little mouse shook his head and looked like he was turning pockets he didn't have out. "Tell him to come in here now."

"He's here already." The kid looked around, then back at him. Jon was having entirely too much fun, he thought, and Larson was going to tell him about it. As soon as this was finished. "You just let my wife go and you'll not be hurt."

"I ain't going to do that, buddy. I need some cash money, and I'm not going to leave here without something to show for it."

There was a noise behind the kid, and Larson looked at Jon as he scurried to the door that led to a closet under the stairs and slipped under the door. Behind him was Carl, who looked as fit as anyone.

When the bat that he'd had in his hands came down on the young man, Virginia fell back on the man too. Carl helped her up and then took her to the couch. Before leaving her to check on the man, Larson kissed her on the mouth and told her not to move.

"Are you all right?" Carl said that he was, but that man wasn't. "No, and you know what? I don't care about him either. He wanted me to give him money."

"Well, you should call the police, Larson. Let them take this piece of trash out." Larson pulled out his cell phone, but for the life of him couldn't remember what he was supposed to do. Carl took the phone from him. "Here you go, young man. You go on over there by that pretty wife of yours, and I'll call them."

~~~

The man was screaming that he was being framed and that he'd been hurt as the police took him away. Carl told them how he'd been taking a nap and heard something upstairs, so he'd come up. Then he told them what he had done, and how he'd only been in the right place at the right time. Joe, the new

162

chief of police, told him that he was glad that he had been. Probably saved some lives. The entire time Carl was talking to the police, her mom held his hand like a lifeline.

After they were gone, Carl sat in the living room with them. He looked a little shaken, but otherwise fine. He did tell them that Jon had called him through a connection he now had, and had him come up as he was unable to make it on time. Virginia knew that to be untrue. Jon had told her several times while the idiot was holding her that he was right behind them and she'd be just fine.

"Well, I'm just glad to have you here. With the baby coming in a while, we'll need to beef up the security around here more." She held onto Larson's hand too while he continued. "What I don't understand is why he just came in the house. Like he lived here or something."

"The blood on his hands is from my friend, T-2. We've decided that his name is Turner and he is well, but not coming now. It would be better for both of us if he were to move further out from here." Virginia told him she was sorry. "No need to be. He agrees that we must at all costs keep this family safe. He's going to find him another person to live with, or live on his own. We have to be careful that not too many of us are around each other. It might cause all of you trouble."

"Does he need money, or anything?" Jon thanked Larson, and told him that he'd taken care that he'd gotten some. "You playing the horses again, young man?"

"Yes, but it is for a good cause." He looked at Carl. "You did a very good thing today, Grandpa Carl. And in the future, you will know how to speak to me and to call to me should you need me, yes?"

"Yes. Startled me out of a nice sleep, but it was well worth it, I have to tell you. I feel better than I have in a great many years." Jon stood up, and so did Carl. "You saved my life. I know that you did it for Flo, and for that, I can't thank you enough...for either. We're going to have a nice life. And even though we've only just met, I feel like I've known her for my entire life. Thank you."

When they were alone again, Virginia sat straddled over Larson's lap. He sat there, staring at her and saying nothing, and she asked him if he was all right. Shrugging, Larson told her he wasn't sure.

"You upset with me or my mom?" Larson said he wasn't, but he was at himself. "And why is that? You were there when I needed you."

"No, Carl was. I was just the man there watching the love of my life having a gun held to her head." She kissed him with all the passion she could muster and sat back up. "Not that I'm complaining, but what was that for?"

"Jon asked me to tell you, but he did this for Carl." Larson asked her if the man with the gun was part of his plan. "No, he was just the reason. He said that Carl has been made to feel useless all his life, and when he asked him to simply come up and guard the back door for him, in case the man got away, he said that he'd take care of him. And I was to let him."

"I see. Are we going to have to have more men coming to our home to make him feel better?" She giggled and told him no, she hoped not. "Good. All I've been able to think about all day was you naked. Riding me. Then Carl showed up. And then there was the thing with Ben. Who, by the way, has decided that he's going to live with us until he kicks up roses. And then this madman tries to make my wife give up her pretty rings."

"I do love them." It was the set from one of the many boxes that they'd found full of jewelry. Holding them up to

164

the light of the fire, she let them sparkle around the room. "I have thought about this a long time, and I want to be a cat, with you. I know that it's painful and all, and that we have to wait until the baby comes, but I want this. Okay?"

"Yes. I'd like that as well. Just to know that you can defend yourself when strange men come into the house and try to make you give them your pretty wedding set." She leaned down to kiss him and he held her to him. "I love you, Virginia. I don't know what I was thinking when I had it in my head that I was going to hate having someone around me all the time."

"I love you as well. And I wanted to thank you for everything you've done for Mom and myself." He kissed her again, unbuttoning her blouse as he held her. "Are we going to have sex right here? On the couch?"

"Yes." He had her buttons open and her bra lifted up over her breast. When he finished suckling at her, he looked at her. "The sooner you're naked and riding me, the sooner I can hear you screaming out my name as you come."

"I love the way that you think."

She pulled her shirt up and over her head. Next came the bra that she'd only just gotten today. He admired it a little before telling her to take it off. By the time she was naked, her pants on the floor with the rest of her clothing, Larson had undone his pants and freed his cock.

"You are so wonderful, hot and thick. Do you have any idea how you make me feel when you're deep inside of me?" He told her to show him. "Gladly."

Slipping over him wasn't as easy as it looked. He had to remove his pants, and she kept getting distracted as he suckled at her breasts. Finally, not able to take much more of his playing, she slammed her body down over his cock and

165

cried out when he filled her fully. His face was tight and she asked him if he was all right.

"Yes, better than all right. I have you surrounding me. Now, darling, ride me." She did, slowly at first, then with more vigor as he cupped his hands around her ass and helped. "Christ, I could come just watching your face as you enjoy yourself. Come for me, baby. I want to watch that expressive face of yours while you do."

She came hard, her body bowed back over his, and she cried out when he touched his thumb to her hard clit. Screaming with a pillow over her face, she fell forward over him. Before she could tell him how fantastic he was, he rolled her to her back and was atop her.

"I love you." She kissed him when he lowered his head to hers. "Come for me again, love. I want to feel you coming all over me."

The climax seemed to explode her. Not just her body, but her mind blinked out, her fingers burned, and even her toes were curling up in a way that made her think that she was having the best sex of her life. But he wasn't finished, and no matter how many times she begged him to stop, he continued taking her to a higher and higher level with each stroke.

This time when he commanded her to come, she felt her body simply freeze. It was as if it were waiting for something. A signal? A new word he might say to her? But nothing could have prepared her for the climax that took her. She was shredded up, nothing in her seemed to work right, and when she let it go, screaming through the entire release, her skin stretched and her mind reached out beyond everything that there was. And it hit her then...she was magical.

The people that had lived and died in the house flashed before her eyes. The furniture being moved was a small blip in her eyes as the woman responsible for them having such nice things was ordering people around.

There was more, so much more that she had a hard time just placing the people. Seeing the things that they touched, moved, and smelled. And when she was able to come back to herself—that was the only way she could think about it... she had come back—her body was limp and Larson was lying atop her, breathing harder than she was.

When he lifted his head and looked at her, all she could do was smile. Nothing in the world could make her feel like this man could. Not even the little boy sleeping in the nursery, nor the child that she carried for him. He was in love with her, and she him. This was what love felt like, and she loved it.

Being carried up to bed later, she noticed that the rooms were dark and wondered briefly about the time. The old grandfather clock that was just down the hall dinged twice, and she giggled a little at how late it was.

"You should have seen your face when I picked you up." She asked him what she'd done. 'You looked sappy. Lovingly sappy."

"Good, that's how you make me feel." He kissed her as he joined her on the bed. "I don't care if I ever wake up. I'm so relaxed right now, you would not believe it."

"I do, I feel the same way. Now hush, go back to sleep. We have a lot going on tomorrow."

She didn't care and yawned. Whatever was going on, they'd just have to do it without her.

167

Chapter 12

Dustin stood back to have a look at the doors he'd hung. He wasn't happy with them, not really. They didn't suit the house. More than that, he thought them just a little over the top with all the etching in them, and wondered why the homeowner would want something like that when they had a beautiful view of the backyard to look at.

As he stood there, he saw something moving out of the corner of his eye and stared at it for several seconds until it moved again. A woman.

Turning slowly, he tried to think if he'd ever met the woman of the house. Or for that matter, any of the occupants other than the man. When he was facing her she stood still, not even moving so much as her hands when he waved at her.

She started toward him after a few seconds. He wasn't sure if he should have been wary of her or not, but she seemed innocent enough. But the closer she got to him, the more worried he got. His cat seemed to have just curled up for a nap when Dustin asked him if this was all right.

"Hello." She nodded. "My name is Dustin McCullough. I

169

don't think I've seen you around here before, have I?"

"I don't think you would have, no." He waited for her to tell him her name, but she looked at the doors that he'd hung. "Those are very ugly."

"Yes, they are." He turned and looked at them, laughing a little. "I had to come and install them today. Apparently, the homeowner really wanted them hung before his family arrives in the morning for Thanksgiving."

"And he wishes to show these off?" He laughed again. She was sort of refreshing. "I would think that he'd hide them. There is no view better than the one that he has right before his eyes. Don't you think?"

"Yes, that's what I was thinking when I saw you. May I ask your name?" She turned and looked at him, but said nothing. "I'm getting sort of nervous here. I don't want to be rude, but I'd like your name, please?"

"I don't have one. I came here because Jon, S-8, said that I'd be safe for a few days." He knew that they'd had some issues yesterday with a man they thought was a friend of Jon's, and this made his cat pissy too. "I can feel him, your other half. I have no desire to hurt you, Dustin. I'm of the lab where he was. Unfortunately, I wasn't able to escape until after the doors were opened some time back. I've been...I think you'd call it drifting for some time now."

"I'm sorry, but I don't have a lot of trust about you. You could be anyone, even someone that has come to kill him." She said that it was impossible to kill him. Or her for that matter. "What is it you've been calling yourself?"

"I was in cage number R-12. I am not as powerful as Jon, but I am powerful." She put out her hand and shifted it into several weapons before letting it drop to her side again. "He's coming here now. As his hawk, the animal that he prefers. He

170

has a brother of yours with him. He has asked that you do not harm me."

"How come they can't speak to me as you are them?" She told him. "Why would you do that? Block me being able to talk to anyone?"

"I do not know you any more than you do me. Correct?" He nodded. "They're here now. With one called Hawk. You are aware that he can shift too?"

"Yes." He watched as his brother and Jon landed on the railing surrounding the deck he was on. When they were both men again, he let his breath out. He hadn't realized just how tense he was until he saw them. "She said that you know her."

"I do. She was in one of the cages that were near mine. I wasn't aware of her until recently. I'm sorry that I didn't warn you she might show up." Dustin told Jon it was all right. "She will need help for a couple of days. And someone to help her hide away."

"You know that you can depend on us." Jon told him that, for right now, it would only be him and Mac knowing that she was here. That the rest of the family would know when she was better. "Why is that? I mean, as a family, we can be so much stronger."

"She doesn't need your strength, Dustin, just a place to rest and to eat some good meals. She has promised not to interfere with your life, but only to rest." Dustin looked at the woman and realized something that he'd not noticed before. She was hurt. "Mac can help her better than most would be able to. Just keep her wounds cleaned and her fed, and she'll be fine."

Dustin wasn't sure about any of this. She was injured, yes, but how had she been hurt? Why him of all the family? Yes, there was Mac being a doctor, but so was Boyd. Then it hit him, and he laughed.

"Is she his mate?" Jon said that he honestly didn't know. "She is, I just know it. Since Hawk didn't react like a man on edge because she's hurt, I can only assume that she is meant for Boyd. And that being—"

"I am standing here. If you would please explain to me what you are talking about, I would be better prepared to participate in the conversation." Dustin told the woman that he was sorry, and explained what he'd been talking about. "I don't know why you'd think such a thing. I'm not even close to being a human. I've been on the run for several months now."

"Neither are we, as I'm sure you know."

She nodded and looked at Jon. "You said that I could rest up and heal. You never mentioned that I'd be mated to someone here."

"I don't know that you are. You couldn't do better should you be mated to these men. They're an amazing bunch, and love like it's their only job." Dustin felt a great deal of pride in what Jon said. Even for someone like him, it was a great compliment to him and his family. "You will be able to rest. And this man's mate is a doctor. She is the best that there is at helping people. Second only to Boyd, these men's brother."

"I will stay with them. But I have no wish to have a man in my life. I have enough trouble keeping me safe." Jon said that he could understand that very well. "When can we leave? I feel weaker by the day."

"Dustin lives not too far from here. He and his family are having a feast of a meal tomorrow." She asked if she'd be required to come. Jon told her no, but she'd be missing out on a great meal. "I shall have to think on it. It's been too long since I've had food in my belly."

The woman looked at the doors again. And when she lifted her hand again, Dustin was sure she was going to shatter the glass. But instead, she simply snapped her fingers and walked toward his truck. Dustin looked at the door, then at Jon.

"What did she do? If anything?" Jon shrugged. "I don't want to have to come out here tomorrow and have to replace these again. I want to eat too much, sit around the living room, and moan about how full I am while I look forward to the next tasty treat. Oh, and watch football with the family."

"You will. I assure you, if I knew what she did, I'd let you know." Dustin went to his truck with Hawk and Jon following. He asked what they'd been doing. "Uncle Hawk is having some issues with transforming himself into things. I was helping him before he went back to his job."

"You'd not believe the shit I can do, Dustin." He laughed when his brother sounded as terrified as he'd ever heard him. As a matter of fact, Dustin hadn't ever heard him be afraid of anything. "Not only can I shift into just about anything—and let me tell you, I mean anything—but I can do shit that makes me kind of scared. I can fucking hold my breath for an hour. Maybe more."

Dustin was still laughing when he got into his truck. The woman was with him, and he looked over at her when both Hawk and Jon disappeared. She smiled at him and he felt it hit him like a rock between the eyes. Christ, she was beautiful.

"You are taking me to your home?" He said that he was and started this truck. Dustin asked her if he could contact his mate now. "Yes. You may reach any of them. Perhaps you can tell me about this mating business that you think is so funny."

"Not funny, but it might be for my brothers. Not Boyd. He's not the humorous type." She asked him if he was a stick in the mud, something she'd heard once. "No, not that either, but he is sort of set in his ways. He has a practice here in town that he shares with my wife. She's Mac."

"I have heard a great deal about her. As well as Boyd. I've been in the area for several weeks now." He nodded as he drove. "I was...I suppose you know that I was created as well. But as I was before Jon, I don't have the same abilities that he does. Not close."

"And you're hurt. How did that happen, if you don't mind me asking?" She told him how she'd been foraging for food when someone tried to harm her. "Harm or rape?"

She stared out the front window, and he wasn't sure she was going to answer him. When she did, he wasn't surprised that she knew what it meant and how the man had been dealt with.

"He wanted me to have relations with him. I told him no, but he wouldn't stop. So, I killed him. But not before he stabbed me several times." She lifted her shirt up and he could see that some of the wounds had already begun to heal, while others were still bleeding. "It has made me weak with it, the loss of blood. I had thought to let it take me, to die, but Jon said that I would still be hunted."

"So, you can be killed." It wasn't a question, but she answered him anyway. That not only could she be killed, but that she was as easy to kill as a human. "I'm sorry about that. I guess we're all like Jon now. And if you are the mate to Boyd, you'll be just as immortal."

"I don't think that I can be his mate." They had pulled into his driveway and he turned to ask her why not. "No one would like to be with someone like me. I'm not human, nor do I have any ability to have children. From what I'm to understand, your kind loves to procreate."

174

"Yes, we do. But that's not a deal breaker when someone loves you. Or at least it shouldn't be." She nodded and got out of the car. "What did you do to the door? The one at the house?"

"No one that sees it will be able to lie to him about how they feel about it. I would like to lie down now, please." He watched her go to the door and knock. He was still standing there when she was let in and the door closed behind her.

Not lie about the door. That could go a lot of different ways, he supposed. But he had a feeling he'd be called out after Thanksgiving to replace it. Smiling, he went into his home. Mac was already fussing over R-12 when he realized she needed a name too.

"R-12, you'll need a name. Something that we can call you that won't draw attention." Mac asked her if she'd heard a name that she liked, or something else she had heard. "It can be most anything. The number will have people asking unwanted questions."

"I will give it some thought. But I do like the fruit peach. Perhaps I can be called something Peach." Mac smiled and he did as well. "I will think more on it."

"Yes, you do that. Anything."

He went to the kitchen to see if he could find anything that might tide him over until dinner. There was a lot going on, so he left with a carrot and a piece of celery. This was no way to treat a man of the house, he thought to himself. And then laughed at his own stupidity. Everyone knew that Mac ruled the home. And he didn't care one bit who knew it.

~~~

Dinner was going to be a grand affair tomorrow. The family was showing up around eleven to help out, and Larson was happy. Terrified out of his mind too, but mostly he was

175

happy. When Virginia joined him in his office, he could tell that she was upset. And the way that she was holding Sam made him smile.

"He's upset with me. Well, not me really, but in general. I think he's upset because when I was putting on his jammies, I caught one of his fingers in it. I cried more than he did." She handed him Sam. "I swear, I'm going to be the worst mother of all times if he plays sports or something. The first time he gets hurt on the field, I'm going to mow people down to get to him." Virginia took the bottle out of her pocket and handed it to him as she sat down.

"How else have you been today? Get any writing done?"

"I did, as a matter of fact. Mom and Carl took Sam for a walk before the temperature started dropping. By the way, I think they're looking for a house of their own. I don't think it's Carl so much as my mom. She wants something of their own." He could understand that and said that to Virginia. "Me too. But I will miss her just being here and knowing that I can go and find her here to talk."

When Sam was finished with his bottle, Larson put him over his shoulder to burp him. When a sound emitted from the little guy, he grimaced. The kid could fill a diaper better than any kid he'd ever seen. And he didn't care for being naked long enough to clean him up either. Standing up, he took him to the nearby changing table—they each had one in their office—and started to strip him down. Sam immediately started to fuss.

"I was wondering about something this morning. And I have to tell you, being awakened with my cock in your mouth was much better than any alarm clock ever invented." She told him he was welcome. "Now, I don't remember what I was going to say to you. Oh yeah, book signing. Do you want to hit a few of them? I think it would be nice to plan a vacation around them."

"I don't like people. I know that I have some fans out there, but I don't think I want them to meet me just yet. I think I should wait awhile." He finished redressing Sam and went to sit with Virginia on the couch. "You do that much better than I do."

"Practice. What is it you think you should wait on? I mean, you're already a best seller. You have emails and posts from people nearly every day. Then there are the ones that beg you to come to their town." She was shaking her head as she took the baby from him. "I got an email from your publisher yesterday."

Her happiness just washed out of her face and was replaced with dread. She held Sam about a foot from her, having stopped in mid motion of cuddling with him when he spoke. Before Larson could say anything more, she started shaking her head and telling him no way.

"I can't do anything like that, Larson. She knows this too. She told me when I first started working with her that she would make sure that no matter what happened, I'd never have to go to any. I'm going to hold her to that." He waited, knowing what her next words were going to be. "I don't want to know what people will say to me."

"Yes, well, she told me to break this part to you gently, but they want to make a movie series, on the big screen, of your books." She handed him the baby and stood up. Larson thought she looked like she was going to be sick. And when she rushed from the room, with her hand over her mouth, he followed her.

He stood outside the bathroom for a few minutes before the nanny came to get Sam. She could hear that Virginia was ill

177

and asked if it was the baby. Nodding, not wanting to tell her what he'd done, he watched the door until it finally opened.

"You call that gently?" He grinned. "I don't think you're the least bit funny right now. And for that matter, I don't even know if I like you."

"You love me, admit it." She growled low and he pulled her into his arms. "I'm sorry, but you had to know that it was going to happen sometime. You're very well liked. And people love your stories."

"They feel sorry for me." He lifted her chin up so that she could see that he was cocking his brow at her. "Well, that's what I want to believe, and you can believe whatever you want. They feel sorry for me."

"All right, love. They feel sorry for you." He held her again and stroked her back as they stood there. "So, these people that feel sorry for you, what do you think they're going to do when they find out your book is going to be made into a big-time movie?"

Before she could retaliate, which he was sure she was going to do later anyway, the front doorbell rang. He loved the sound. It wasn't a usual ring, like most houses, but a minute of classical music, complete with harps and all.

Making his way to the door with Virginia at his side, he waited for Ben to answer it and stood back when he didn't recognize the person standing there. The elderly woman smiled at Ben and asked if Larson was at home.

"Mr. and Mrs. McCullough are both at home, miss. May I tell them who is calling?" She said her name, but Larson didn't hear it. "If you'd come this way, miss, I'll go and tell Mr. McCullough that you are here."

He turned then and saw them both standing there and told them who she was. Just as her name registered with him, two other people entered the room, one a willowy blonde girl, the other a dark-haired boy. Both of them were dressed in somber clothing, and he knew why now.

"You're Tom and Donna's children. Come in, come in." They hugged him, and he hugged them back. Mrs. Simmons, Tom's mom, hugged him and Virginia twice before she pulled a pretty hanky from her pocket and wiped at her tears. "I'm so sorry about your loss, Mrs. Simmons, children. Tom and Donna were good people."

"Yes, they were. And the best parents anyone could have had." The girl, Jenny, smiled at him. "He told us to come here if something happened to them. I don't know why he thought something would, but we have something for you."

"My dad and mom, they wrote us a letter when they left. Gave it to Grandma in case they were hurt or came up missing." Vince, the younger of the two children, handed him a thick envelope. "We read it over, my sister and me. And my dad, he had it right about you. He said that you'd figure things out and fix it for us."

"You mean finding their killer?" Vince nodded and leaned into his grandma. He was taller than her, but she hugged him like he was just a little boy. Larson thought it was something they'd been doing his entire life. "I was glad to do so. But it wasn't just me, it was my entire family that helped."

"My son, he thought the world of you. And he told me that if something happened to him and Donna, we were to come to you and give you this. I miss him more and more every day. And the kids, they've been my only saving grace." She cried a little more, and Virginia held her as she led them into the living room. "I'm sorry. We probably could have waited until after Thanksgiving, but the kids wanted to come now. To do what their parents wanted them to."

179

Ben brought them in some refreshments and asked if they'd be joining them for dinner, there was plenty. Virginia said that they would, and Rose, Tom's mom, insisted they could find them something on the way back to the hotel.

"Nonsense. You'll stay for dinner. And for tomorrow as well. In fact, we've only just gotten all the bedrooms furnished over the last few days, and you can stay here." Virginia told Ben to make arrangements to have their things brought here. "Now. You'll not say no. You can ask my mom, I'm very pushy about things in order to get my way."

"You two are so sweet." Rose looked at him and the envelope that he'd yet to open. "Tom, we had a long talk before he left. He didn't tell me what was going on, but he did say that should something happen to him or Donna, we were to lay low until the time was right. I had no idea what he meant until that came for us. It's the check, the one that you sent him that day. It's signed and all by them both. And he told me to bring it here, to you."

"He didn't tell me anything. Other than have me sell the shares to his stock in Ranger Mountain. Once that was done, he told me that he'd bought a boat. That he and Donna were looking forward to sailing with the kids this coming summer." She nodded, and Jenny held her brothers hand. "I'm so sorry about this. I wish I could have talked him out of going."

"I don't believe that you could have, young man. He was set on this and excited for it. Donna too." Rose wiped at her nose again. "I find that I can get through almost a whole hour now without sobbing about my losses. But that…he said in a letter that I got a couple days after he was found dead, that we were to come to you and you'd know what to do with that money. Also, that you'd not leave anything to chance, that if something did happen, you'd make sure justice was served."

"Thank you." He opened the envelope that was addressed to him. "He wants me to take the money that he sent you and invest it for your future. And to help you both get into a good college."

"He said that you'd be able to turn that into some money so that the kids wouldn't have to work." Larson told Rose that he'd do just that. "Thank you, Larson. As I said, he thought the world of you and what you'd done for him. When I think back on that conversation that we had just before he left, I ache with it. I think he knew, and somehow figured that being on the boat without the children, it would be better."

Dinner wasn't as it usually was, noisy and loud. But the kids did eat, and they spoke to them when talked to. Virginia told them about the dinner that was going to be here tomorrow, as well as all the people that were going to be there.

"Don't think I won't be keeping an eye on you to be sure you eat." Jenny nodded and played with her chicken. Larson wasn't sure what she was going to say next when a crying Sam was brought to her. "My son has the temperament of a wart hog."

They all laughed and Jenny asked to hold him. After that, things seemed to loosen up, and laughter seemed to ring around the table again. Sam, of course, was eating up all the attention, and it seemed to Larson that he was flirting with Jenny. Larson was happier about Sam being upset than he had been about anything in a while. Then the nanny winked at him as she left them for her own supper.

My goodness, he thought, the entire household was helping with these children. After that, Larson joined them in teasing each other. He could not wait until tomorrow.

Chapter 13

Boyd was having the time of his life. He'd just brought a brand-new person into the world and couldn't stop smiling. After four little girls, Mr. Patterson had his son. And what a son he turned out to be. Ten pounds and four ounces.

"Look at him, will you?" Brad smiled at him over his wife nursing their newest addition. "Can you believe that? I'm a father of a big boy. He's going to play linebacker or something equally exciting. And we're going to be there for every play. Aren't we, honey?"

Not that he wasn't there for his girls. The reason he'd been almost too late to see his son coming into the world was that he had taken his oldest daughter to baseball tryouts, where she'd made the team.

Another of his girls was a gymnast. The third one, only about three, was quite the swimmer. And the fourth daughter was already playing better ball than most of the adults that helped coach her. And not once had he ever pushed them into what they loved doing. Brad just stood back and let them do whatever they wanted, so long as they gave it their best.

"Have you got a name for this fellow yet?" He nodded and laughed. "I'm sure this is going to be good. How long did your wife argue with you before you bullied her into it?"

"It's her pick. I told her it could be." Boyd looked at his patient, who was smiling like she'd won the lottery. Boyd thought in a way that she had. "I told her that she got to name this one, no matter what we had. And it was going to be the last. I can barely afford these girls."

Which wasn't true. Brad, like a lot of people in town, had gone to Larson about helping turn their money into gold. Brad was a wealthy man, and could afford anything and everything that his children wanted.

"His name is Bradley William Patterson, the second. We'll call him Will." Boyd looked at the shocked look on her husband's face as he checked on the baby again. "You said I could name him anything I wanted. Well, I wanted him named for the greatest man I know. You."

"You said you hated my full name. Made fun of me when I suggested it for our first child." She laughed and told him that was how she had been able to surprise him. "I see. So, you've been waiting on this day forever to name our son after me?"

"I have. I knew that one of these days we'd have ourselves a son, and that he'd be just like his daddy. Almost as big too, as it turned out." They were laughing as Boyd gave Will a clean bill of health and sent him on to the nursery. As soon as Vicki was ready for her room, he made arrangements to head to his brother's house. Thanksgiving was the best day there was.

On the drive to the house, he made verbal notes on his recorder so that he'd not forget anything on his day off. He was on call, but the office was closed up. And thanks to the

Pattersons having their baby a day early, he was free of being called in on that as well. Sitting at the light at the intersection, he sent the notes to the service that would not only type them up for him, but also make sure they were put in the patient's notes.

Boyd looked around while he waited for the light to change. The little town was gearing up for the next holiday. There were people working in a couple of shops now, putting up trees in their front windows. One store was painting a scene in theirs. He knew that since he'd been a little boy, the Wilsons had been having a whimsical painting done every year. And he was glad that the new owners were doing the same thing.

Looking at the light to make sure that he hadn't missed it, he saw a man walking the streets without a coat or hat. When the light turned finally, he drove forward and pulled over when he realized that the man wasn't stopping. Getting out of his car, he slowly approached the man, talking as he did so.

"Sir? Are you all right? Do you need me to call someone?" He turned and looked at him then, and he knew who he as. The very man that he'd been thinking about. "Mr. Wilson, what's going on? Why are you out here without a coat?"

"I have to set up the store. I didn't know it was Thanksgiving today, and I have to get the store ready." He led him to his car, looking around for anyone that might be looking for him. "They said today was a special day. I didn't know what they meant until I got two pieces of pumpkin pie for dessert. It's Thanksgiving. I have to set up the store for tomorrow. It's our biggest day. Is your mom gonna bring you by to see Santa, Boyd?"

"I don't think she will this year. But I'll bring her by." He said that was good. After getting him in the car and buckling

185

him in, Boyd pulled out his cell and called the police. "Mr. Wilson was just wandering the streets."

"We've been looking for him for the past hour, Boyd. Christ, thanks for calling us. I'll call the home and let them know. Poor old man. His wife passed a few months ago, and he didn't take it well." He said he could understand that. Joe said he could as well. "I'll be by to get him. You might have to sit with him a bit, is that okay? We're short staffed today."

"I'll take him to my brother's house. We'll make sure he's warm and fed. There are a lot of people going to be there this year." Joe told him that his own wife was there, and he was coming by after work. "Just get him then. And we'll keep him safe. Is that all right?"

"More than all right. You McCulloughs, you guys are the best." Joe laughed a little. "I sure hope that when I get old and infirm, there is someone out there like you for me. No telling what sort of trouble I can get into when I'm as old as Mr. Wilson."

Boyd said nothing, not commenting on the fact that he'd not be getting old and would, in all likelihood, still be practicing medicine when Joe was long gone. It saddened him, and made him realize how lonely it would be when everyone around him, friends and all, would be gone and he'd still be taking care of their great-great-great-great grandchildren.

As he drove them to Larson's he thought of his life so far. He was happy with it. Boyd had a good family, a home now, and he had lots of nieces and nephews around all the time. With him and Hawk the only single men in the family, they hung out more. Commiserated on how domesticated their other brothers were. He loved their wives, had fun with them, but his mate, he knew, wasn't going to come.

"I had my chance, Mr. Wilson, and I let it go for the

pursuit of a career." Mr. Wilson told him that there wasn't anything like a good woman. "Yes, my brothers have great wives. My dad and mom have been happily married for a very long time. I love them to pieces, but it's not in my cards to be as happy as them."

"Only you can make yourself happy, young man. There ain't nothing out there that can make you what you want to be but for yourself." Boyd nodded, not sure he didn't have it right. "Why just the other day, the missus and I were talking about you boys and how well you've turned out to be. That other one, the bird? Anyway, I worry for him a lot. Poor boy will need himself a good strong woman to tame his heart. And you, you need someone to shake you up a bit. Rock your world like that Lauren does for Colin."

"You know Lauren?" He said she came to see him sometimes. "Well, I didn't know that. She is a world breaker."

"That ain't all she is breaking, either." They both laughed about that. "I tell you, meeting you today was a God send. I been cooped up for so long that I can't be around people like them old ones there anymore. I know that I get lost sometimes, used to even before the kids locked me away to forget, but I got good days too, and I'm having one with you today. You're a good boy, Boyd. Don't have enough people telling me that anymore."

"I've always thought you were a good man. And a good husband and father. You provided for your children all their lives, Mr. Wilson. And you made that little store the highlight of my childhood when I was growing up. Going there with our mom at this time of year was something that my brothers and I looked forward to all year." He smiled and nodded, and wiped at his tears. "You're a good man. And I'm glad to have known you all my life."

187

"Thank you. Thank you very much. Now, let's not be melancholy on this day. It's my favorite holiday, next to my birthday. Though, I've not looked forward to that in a great many years either. Going to be ninety-four. Can you believe it?" He laughed heartily. "My mom said the way I was as a kid, I'd be lucky if I made it to my twenties. I sure do miss her. She had a mean smack when you needed it, and the most loving hug a boy or man could ever need. You still hug your mom, Boyd?"

"I do. And my dad and brothers too. Not too much the women in the family, not the mates, but I love them as well." He said that was a good thing too. "Yes. I love all the kids too. You ready for this?"

"I believe I am. Yes, sir, I do believe I am." They pulled up in front of the house and his dad came out. He wondered how he knew that he was bringing a guest, and figured that Joe would have called and told them. "Well, if it ain't Richard McCullough. You still taking candy that you ain't paid for?"

"That was nearly fifty years ago, you old coot. And I came back and paid you. I told you then and I'm telling you now, I didn't remember having it in my hand." They were laughing as they made their way into the house. Boyd parked his car with the rest of them and went to the door too. Life was treating them pretty well at the moment, and he was going to enjoy it. He had a feeling that things were about to be topsy turvy again soon.

The house was full to capacity. There were strangers there, as well as old friends. This is what it was supposed to be like, he thought. Opening your doors to everyone that wanted to come visit. Having a grand meal and lots of conversation. To him, this was all he needed.

"You ready for the coming year?" He asked Hawk what

he meant, just noticing that he wasn't in fatigues. "I'm not going back after the holidays. I've decided to come home and open my own business in training people how to defend themselves."

"Really? You're not going to go away for long periods anymore?" He said that he'd had enough, and that he still might leave when it got to be too much. "I'm glad. I've been out to see your house. Could you get any more off the beaten path?"

"Yeah, when Dustin told me about the house, all I could think about was having four walls around me, and that would have driven me nuts. But I love the place. Open plan in the lower levels, and the bedrooms are huge. I haven't gotten much in the way of stuff to put it in yet, but I have plenty of time. How about you?"

"I have a nice little house. Nothing like you guys. It's only me, you know." Hawk said he was sorry. "Don't. Not today, okay? Let's not talk about mates and losses today. I don't think I could take it."

"Yeah, okay. Have you told anyone, besides me?" Boyd shook his head and said that he'd not. "Well, I'd at least tell Dad. He'll tell everyone, then you won't have to worry about them shoving women at you every ten minutes."

They were laughing when dinner was called. As he entered the huge dining room he marveled at first the size of it, then the beauty. Larson had said that he'd done some improvements on the place, and it looked amazing. The table, however, wasn't nearly big enough for them all, and there was some ribbing at Larson for not thinking ahead.

"Oh, but I did. The people at the table will be served, the rest of you are going to be out of luck." There was a playful rush to the table and he opened the doors to the deck. "Nah,

I was joking. But I did think ahead. Guys, your table awaits."

The deck at this side of the house was enclosed, with windows for the warmer months. The room was as toasty warm as the dining room, and once the doors were opened, it looked like a massive room. Sitting at the outdoor table, Boyd fell in love with the big house. He might just be looking for one in the future.

~~~

Trying on names was a lot different than trying on clothing, she soon discovered. While the family was away, she watched television. The remote wasn't really all that complicated, but she only had to move around the stations with her mind. But she held it in her hand while she did this so as not to give away some of her secrets.

They're trustworthy. She smiled at Jon's voice. *You don't have to hide when you're here. They're very accepting and generous with their friendship and help when you need it. They're not like the people that we used to have to endure.*

Do they know all about you? He told her that for the most part he was still learning what he could do, but yes, they knew it all. *And that you've changed them, do they know that?*

Yes. And while some are very happy with the idea, there are a couple that aren't so sure. My blood is very powerful, and it can kill too. She said that she'd not been given anything like him. *No one has. I'm different, more so than even the people at the lab know.*

I'm older than you are as well. Even older than the man that they call Father. Do they need to know that? He said that it wouldn't be important to them, but yes, they should know. *I have so much to say, I think. They're going to wish they'd never met me, Jon. What will I do then? Leave and start again?*

You were a test subject, the same as me. You were the seed while I was the plant; that is the only difference between us. She said

190

she wasn't so sure. *I am. Have you picked a name yet? It's very important, as we said, but it can be fun as well. I've had two now. My name from the lab was S-8, which was changed to Savage. But now I'm a McCullough.*

I have not. I've been watching the television. There is a lot of violence in the world now, isn't there? I was in the lab for so long, I missed a great many things going on. Now I wish I hadn't bothered looking. It's a frightening place here. He said that it had been, but he was safe now. *They say that too. You're safe. Or you'll be safe. I don't even know what that means.*

It means that every waking breath, you don't have to worry that someone will come for you. Cut into you for things that you were born with. And that you can be warm when you need it, get a hug or even just enjoy them. They are a loud and comical group. But they can be just as deadly when necessary.

As am I. And you for that matter. We were made this way. I was just a lowly witch. Nothing bothered me. Until one day a man came and took me away from all that I loved. Put me into a locked cage and made me have sex with everything and anything. I was ruined for any other person in the world after that. He told her he was sorry. *They put things into me. Chemicals and other creatures' blood. They made me this way, and then were surprised when I fought back, using the same powers that they wanted from me.*

You have suffered enough, I think. Now you can be safe. So long as you do what I told you. You must be careful. She asked him why he bothered with her. *Because you were a victim, just as I was. Perhaps not the same way nor in the same lab, but just as badly. Tomorrow, I will explain to them what has happened to you, and you'll see that they're not going to care.*

This mating thing. Do you suppose they really think that I'm to belong to one of them? I have no desire to, Jon. It's hard to think of anyone wanting me without some kind of agenda. He told her

191

that she'd be so loved, it would make her smile more than ever before. *I don't have that in me any longer. I'm used up and dead inside.*

If that were true, you'd not be in that lovely home with nice people watching television, trying to find yourself a new name to please them. She turned off the set and heard him laugh at her. *You are so predictable. I think I have a name you can try on. How about you call yourself Sandra? It means helper of mankind. I think that suits you. Or even Sandy. I think either of them will work.*

She liked it. It was simple and easy to say. She even liked the meaning of the world. It made her sound as if she might have worth. Not that she did, but the name Sandra did. As she said it over and over again, Sandra liked it even more.

There you go. One less thing you have to worry about. I think, as I said, that it suits you. Is there anything else I can do for you this fine day? She told him he could leave her alone. *Nay, my sister, I cannot do that. You are mine to protect, just as the rest of them are. And you won't be able to not love them. They're wonderfully amazing.*

She moved around the room once she had her name and touched some of the objects there. A picture of a cherubic baby. There was a little bottle of sand on a stand. Sandra loved the old furniture in the house. It was a beautiful mixture of old and new. Touching things, she could feel what it had suffered, where it had been, and who else had touched it.

When darkness began to settle around the house, she made her way to the deck and sat in the chair there. Since the deck was covered, it was cooler than it might have been outside of it, but there wasn't any snow on the furniture, nor did she have to worry about her prints showing up on the decking floor.

Just as she was settling down for a little while she saw

the wolves, natural to this part of the state, moving around the yard. Also, some deer came out to play, and neither of the two natural enemies seemed to mind each other. It occurred to her that they might not be natural wolves, and watched them play in the snow.

At darkness, she went into the house. There was a fireplace in the room she had come into, and she lit it with her magic. There wasn't any way for her to have gone out to the woodpile at the back of the property, not without startling the other animals, so she brought it to her.

Just as she was bringing in the last armload, she saw the two men standing at the edge of the property. One she knew to be a McCullough. He was stout like Dustin, and seemed to have the same hair color. The other man, bigger than the McCulloughs, had his back to her, but she was sure they weren't related. It took her several minutes of watching them before she remembered that she was hiding out and made her way into the house. She kept an eye on the two men.

When McCullough started to turn away, the bigger man grabbed for him. It was scary for her, to see them together, and Sandra wasn't even sure why. But when McCullough fell to the ground, his body limp after hitting it, she shifted to a small bird to help. As soon as she saw the gun, she landed on the big man and clawed deep into his bare head.

It took her ten minutes of dodging and swooping down at the man and his gun before he finally fell back on the ground. Almost as soon as he was down, he was up and running away. She was afraid of him, that he might come back, when she turned back to herself to check on McCullough. The snow was stained with his blood, and she thought that his arm might be broken from the rock he'd landed on.

As soon as she touched his arm, he opened his eyes and

stared at her. She asked him if he was all right. He nodded, then moaned with the movement.

"It's hard to tell, I think." She helped him sit up, careful of his arm. "If I shift, is it going to upset you?"

"No, since that is how I got here to assist you." He nodded, but only laid back on the snow. The wolves that had been around the property earlier came toward them, and she had to shoo them away when they got too close. "Go away. Don't you see that he's been hurt?"

"They're the pack that roams around here. They're making sure I'm not going to be harmed by you. They can smell that you're not human." She watched them as they ran to the man and licked his face. "I'm going to shift now."

He went from man to cat in seconds. It was a beautiful jaguar, and his fur looked shiny soft. It was all she could do not to touch him, to allow her fingers to run though his fur to see if it was as soft as it looked. When he turned back to a man, she was surprised to see that he was fully dressed. His wounds were gone as well, and his arm looked to have mended properly.

"My name is Boyd." She remembered them talking about him. He was a doctor. "I'm guessing that you're not from around here."

"No. I guess sort of. I've been at the lab, and then since I escaped from there, I have been roaming the countryside. It's beautiful, and has grown up so much since I was captured." He nodded and stood up. She was glad for it; he was much taller than she'd thought he was. "That man, he meant to kill you."

"Yes, but he was not going to be able to. He wanted something and I don't have it." She asked him if he was going to get it for him. "No. I don't think I will. I think he's looking

194

for you."

"Me?" She looked back the way the man had gone and was suddenly very afraid. "I don't know why he'd want me. I'm just a regular person."

"I don't doubt that, but you're also a friend of Jon's, and someone like him. But not quite, correct?" She shook her head and wanted to cry. "Don't cry, we'll keep you safe."

"They said I was your mate. The others. I don't think that we'd work out as one, do you? But it matters little now. I have to be going. Jon told me that I'd be safe here so long as I was careful. But how could I have stayed back when you were hurt? I couldn't. So now here I am, on the run again, and I've only just gotten a name. And now I have to go—"

He put his hand over her mouth, and she realized that she'd been talking a great deal. And she, for the life of her, couldn't remember what she'd said. Instead of telling him that, she watched his face for any sign that he wasn't happy.

"First of all, you're not my mate. Not that it matters on the large scheme of things, but there you have it. I had one once, but I was too stupid to realize that life goes on and things happen." She had no idea what he was talking about, but she let him speak. "You are safe here. The man that was here? He doesn't even know what you look like, nor what sex you are. He is just looking for someone magical."

"How did he know to come here?" He told her that since they were cats, he figured that they had an inside peg on everything. "What a stupid man. How would that even work?"

"I don't know either. But that's why you're going to be safe." He looked back at the wooded area around them. "Have you eaten yet? My mom ordered this fantastic dinner, and there are tons of leftovers. How about you come back this way with me, meet my overbearing family, and have some great food?"

"I should go back to the house and wait for Dustin." He asked her why she was at his house. "I don't know. Jon told me to go there, and that I could rest and be healed. I have been hurt. Jon thought that should I need extra help, there was a doctor there that might be able to help me. I don't know why he didn't send me to you."

"More than likely, he thought if we were mates that you and I wouldn't make it to dinner." He started to lead her back through the woods when it occurred to her what he meant. Sandra asked him about it. "Just what you're thinking. I'd not be able to stop from having my way with you. But, as I said, I've lost my mate, and while you're a very lovely woman, I had my chance and messed it up."

By the time they were at the big house, she decided that she wished that he was her mate. He was a kind and funny man. She supposed that she couldn't be as lucky as to have a mate in the first place, much less one like this one.

Before You Go...

HELP AN AUTHOR

write a review

THANK YOU!

Share your voice and help guide other readers to these wonderful books. Even if it's only a line or two your reviews help readers discover the author's books so they can continue creating stories that you'll love. Login to your favorite retailer and leave a review. Thank you.

Kathi Barton, winner of the Pinnacle Book Achievement award as well as a best-selling author on Amazon and All Romance books, lives in Nashport, Ohio with her husband Paul. When not creating new worlds and romance, Kathi and her husband enjoy camping and going to auctions. She can also be seen at county fairs with her husband who is an artist and potter.

Her muse, a cross between Jimmy Stewart and Hugh Jackman, brings her stories to life for her readers in a way that has them coming back time and again for more. Her favorite genre is paranormal romance with a great deal of spice. You can visit Kathi online and drop her an email if you'd like. She loves hearing from her fans. aaronskiss@gmail.com.

Follow Kathi on her blog: http://kathisbartonauthor.blogspot.com/

www.ingramcontent.com/pod-product-compliance
Lightning Source LLC
Chambersburg PA
CBHW032134170626
46808CB00006B/2226

9 781629 898308